# TAKAOKA'S

## TRAVELS

# TAKAOKA'S TRAVELS

Tatsuhiko Shibusawa

*translated by David Boyd*

Stone Bridge Press • *Berkeley, California*

*Published by*
Stone Bridge Press
P.O. Box 8208, Berkeley, CA 94707
sbp@stonebridge.com • www.stonebridge.com

This publication has received the William F. Sibley Memorial Subvention Award for Japanese Translation from the University of Chicago Center for East Asian Studies Committee on Japanese Studies.

The MONKEY imprint was established by Stone Bridge Press in partnership with MONKEY New Writing from Japan.

Cover design by Counterpunch Inc. / Nicholas Vitacco. Cover image sources: *Tiger in Wind*, after Maruyama Ōkyo (1733–1773), Cleveland Museum of Art; [on cover and endpapers] *Chinese Landscape: summer*, Kanō Tan'yū (1602–1674), National Museum of Asian Art, Smithsonian.

Printed in the United States of America.

p-ISBN 979-8-9886887-0-9 (paperback)
p-ISBN 979-8-9886887-2-3 (casebound)
e-ISBN 979-8-9886887-1-6 (ebook)

# CONTENTS

# TAKAOKA'S
## TRAVELS

# DUGONG

On the twenty-seventh day of the first month in the sixth year of the Xiantong era, Prince Takaoka set sail from Guangzhou on a ship bound for Hindustan. By the Japanese calendar the year was Jōgan 7, and the Prince was sixty-five. At his side were two monks from Japan, Anten and Engaku, both of whom had accompanied the Prince during his time in Tang.

Guangzhou was one of the liveliest ports along the South Sea, rivaling even Jiaozhou, or Lūqīn, as it was known to the Arabs. As far back as the Han dynasty, when it was known as Panyu, the port of Guangzhou traded in a great many precious goods: rhinoceros horn, elephant ivory, tortoiseshell, pearls, jade, silver, bronze, amber, aloeswood, cardamom, and more. In Xiantong 6, the port was as vibrant as ever. Moored cheek by jowl were ships from Hindustan, Arabia, Sinhala, Persia—there were even Kunlun boats from the Southern Lands. The men of the port were no less exotic, with eyes and skin of all shades and colors. Suntanned sailors stripped to the waist bounded across the decks in a veritable showcase of the world's races. Although it would still be four centuries before Marco Polo or Odoric would travel to this part of the globe, there were already white savages on some of the ships. Even for the spectacle of the strange people passing through, the port of Guangzhou was a wonder to behold.

In broad strokes, the Prince's plan was to leave this port aboard a small ship and head southwest via the route known as the Guangzhou–Haiyi Road. He and his companions would then disembark in Jiaozhou, the heart of the Protectorate of Annan, whereupon they would follow the Annan–Hindustan Road to their destination. But this road was forked: One path led over the mountains of Annan toward Funan in the south, and the other wound through Kunming and cut across the Dali

Plain, ending in Pyu to the southwest. The Prince and his men had yet to decide which path they would take. Moreover, it was not out of the question to continue the voyage by sea. Sailing past the coasts of Champa, Chenla, and Panpan on the Malay Peninsula, they could round the Cape of Luoyue and enter the Indian Ocean through the Strait of Malacca. But whether going by land or by sea, all routes harbored unforeseeable dangers. Thus, little could be gained by planning ahead. For now, the Prince and his fellow monks would cast their fates to the wind and go as far south as possible. There was no need to think any further than that.

It is never very cold near the equator, even at the height of winter, and the wind was warm. Prince Takaoka stood on the deck, his back straight as ever. He was well into his sixties but appeared at least ten years younger. As he looked out over the bustling port from which they were about to depart, a child slipped between the legs of the men carrying cargo. The Prince and Anten both spotted the boy as he made his way onto the ship, and exchanged puzzled looks. Like the Prince, Anten had the bearing of a contemplative monk, but he was a sharp-eyed, brawny man of about forty years.

"Mere moments until our departure and an unexpected visitor drops in on us!"

"I'll go and have a look, Miko."

The boy who was dragged before the Prince had bright cheeks and delicate limbs like a girl. Right away, Anten began to question him in the local language. Despite his appearance, Anten was in fact a highly skilled linguist who regularly served as the Prince's interpreter. The boy gasped for breath as he explained: "I'm a slave and I've run away from my master. Should my pursuers find me, they will almost certainly kill me.

I seek shelter for but a moment. If this ship were to set sail for some remote place, however, so be it. I would not regret leaving this land, not in the least. If you should allow me to stay and bail bilgewater, I would be grateful beyond words."

Such was the boy's earnest plea.

The Prince looked to Anten and said:

"It would seem that a little bird in need has flown into our arms. How can we turn him away? Let's bring the child with us."

At this, Anten voiced his concern:

"As long as he doesn't slow us down. . . . If you wish it, Miko, I suppose I have no objection."

Then Engaku joined in:

"We could never be so cruel as to abandon him. This is a voyage to Holy Hindustan, after all. It must be the Buddha's will."

Just as the three monks had reached an agreement, the shipmaster yelled from the stern:

"Unmoor! Hard to starboard!"

As the ship slid slowly into the heart of the bay, two or three men on the wharf who appeared to be searching for the slave boy shouted in their direction. Overjoyed at narrowly escaping with his life, the boy threw himself at the Prince's feet, choking on tears. The Prince took the boy by the hand and said:

"I will call you Akimaru. Until a few years ago, I had a page by that name who fell to the plague back in Chang'an. You can be my second Akimaru."

In this way, the Prince's entourage grew to three: Anten, Engaku, and young Akimaru. Engaku, by the way, was five years Anten's junior. He was a polymath, well versed in Daoist medicine and herbalism, and his encyclopedic knowledge had won him the Prince's respect on numerous occasions.

The ship set sail for the Leizhou Peninsula and Hainan Island. It drifted across the open sea like a solitary leaf, speeding and slowing as the wind willed. At times, the water seemed still as oil. . . . Was the ship moving or simply floating in place? At other times, the ship was blasted across the water at such a speed that it seemed the vessel would surely blow apart. It was as though the wind and waves in these parts had some sort of mysterious power, a force that no ship could possibly resist. Every day, like clockwork, terrible squalls buffeted the ship, encompassing the travelers in curtains of slate-gray rain and making it impossible to tell sky from sea; at times, the ship seemed to be flying through the air. Struck by the mystique of the ocean, the Prince said, to no one but himself:

"As we head south, things will occur that we could never have imagined back in Japan. Perhaps the world itself will turn upside-down! But I mustn't be alarmed. As we approach Hindustan, things will only become stranger and stranger. And isn't that exactly what I wanted? Hindustan approaches! Rejoice! Soon it will be within my grasp."

At the prow of the small ship, the Prince was showered by spindrift as he spoke. His words, spat out into the darkness, were snatched up by the wind and broke into pieces as they tumbled across the sea.

THE PRINCE WAS A child, no older than five or six, when he first heard of Hindustan. The name made him quiver with sweet intoxication. It was a philter to the boy. None other than his father's consort, Fujiwara no Kusuko, had whispered those three syllables in his ear at night.

Before the Prince's father came to be known as Emperor Heizei, Kusuko and her daughter had entered the Eastern

Palace as attendants. In no time, Kusuko apparently stole the Crown Prince's heart, and when he later ascended to the throne, their attachment became increasingly evident, despite Kusuko already being a married woman. Those years saw the height of Kusuko's favor. Night after night, she shared a bed with the Emperor. There were rumors that Kusuko had beguiled him, though she remained unshaken by the scandal. At the time, the Emperor was thirty, at the peak of his manhood. No one knows how old Kusuko was. We do know that she had a daughter whom she had intended to present to the court for marriage to the Crown Prince, which meant her daughter had to have been of marriageable age. Thus Kusuko was likely somewhat older than her lover. And yet she didn't seem to age. It was curious how perfectly she retained the radiant beauty of youth. As suggested by the name Kusuko, which contains the character for medicine, she had a profound knowledge of traditional herbs; she was no less an expert in the art of lovemaking. And, if the rumors were true, she drank cinnabar and made use of secret arts to maintain her appearance.

We also know that, at the time, the word "kusuko" was used as a common noun to refer to poison-tasters. That this word would become Kusuko's name tells us much about her character.

As it happens, it was also during the reign of Emperor Heizei that the hundred-volume herbalist text *Formulae of the Daidō Era* was compiled. Medicines and poisons, we must not forget, played a crucial role in the power struggles of the day.

Emperor Heizei was very fond of his young son. He often took him out with Kusuko on trips to the nearby mountains. In court and at home, the Emperor often allowed Kusuko and the young Prince to remain in his company. Unbeknownst to the Prince's mother, the boy often stayed at Kusuko's home with his

father. Kusuko didn't need to endear herself to the boy. She easily won his heart, and the two settled into the sort of closeness
often enjoyed by partners in crime, as if they were sharing some
secret. On occasion, when the Emperor had to attend to an
official matter, Kusuko chose to sleep beside the Prince. Lying
next to him, Kusuko told him all kinds of stories, animating his
young dreams.

"Can you tell me the name of the realm beyond the sea,
Miko?"

"Koryŏ."

"Right, Koryŏ. And what about the one beyond that?"

"Tang."

"Tang. Right again. They also call it Cīnasthāna. And then
comes?"

"I don't know . . ."

"Really? Far, far beyond Tang, there's a land called
Hindustan."

"Hindustan . . ."

"Right. The land where the Buddha was born. In Hindustan, there are fantastic animals in the fields, curious plants in
the gardens, and celestial beings in the sky. And that's not all.
Everything in Hindustan is the opposite of what it is in the
world we know. Our day is their night, our summer is their winter, our up is their down, our man is their woman. In Hindustan,
rivers run backward, and mountains sink deep into the earth
like massive holes. What do you think, Miko? Can you imagine
so strange a place?"

Kusuko loosened her silk kimono as she spoke, revealing
a breast. She took the Prince's hand and placed it on her chest.
This had been a custom of theirs for some time. Kusuko would
smile and slip her hand between the Prince's legs, cupping his

testicles, rolling them around like a pair of Baoding balls. The Prince was in ecstasy but remained perfectly quiet, allowing everything to happen as Kusuko willed. Were it not Kusuko— had it been one of the many other women serving at the palace—the Prince would surely have shuddered in disgust and pushed her away. That this never happened only shows that, as indecent as it may sound, there was not a hint of coquetry or debauchery in what Kusuko did.

"Miko, I believe you'll grow up and take a ship to Hindustan. No, I'm almost sure of it. I can see the future. But I'll be long dead by then—no longer a part of this world."

"What? Why?"

"I can't say, but I know I'll die soon. I can see it in the mirror of my heart."

"But you're so young, Kusuko!"

"Oh, Miko, you say the kindest things. But I'm not afraid of dying. My soul will move on. I'm tired of being human anyway. In my next life, I think I'd like to hatch—"

"From an egg?" the Prince interrupted.

"Yes, like a bird or a snake. Doesn't that sound nice?"

Kusuko stood up. She took something bright from her bedside cabinet and threw it across the dark courtyard, then said, as if singing:

"Away, away you go! Off to distant Hindustan!"

The Prince's eyes lit up as he watched her.

"What was that? What did you throw? Please tell me!"

Kusuko laughed. "Something that will make its way to Hindustan. After fifty years in the moonlight of the jungle, I'll be reborn from it as a bird."

But the Prince was unsatisfied. He persisted:

"But what was that thing? That glowing ball!"

"Hm, I wonder. Why don't we call it the egg of my rebirth? Or, it being mine, we might call it a medicine ball. . . . Really, I have no idea what to call it. The world is full of such things, Miko."

That image of Kusuko was burned into the Prince's memory, like a figure in a shadow play. A woman on a moonlit veranda, tossing a small ball of light into the darkness. Polished like a jewel over the years, the memory came to shine even more brilliantly with the passage of time. Had it really taken place? Was it only a dream? As he got older, even the Prince wanted to doubt the authenticity of his memory, but something wouldn't let him. Whenever he thought about it, he told himself there was no way his recollection of that night could be so clear were there not some degree of truth to it.

What she said to him that night haunted him like a riddle. But only four years later, in the fall of the year Daidō 5, a struggle broke out between those who stood with the retired emperor, the Prince's father, and those who sided with the sitting emperor. Kusuko took her own life amid the chaos, and that shook the Prince to his core. Kusuko had been with the retired emperor when his camp moved on Emperor Saga. She shared a palanquin with him as they advanced east from Sentō Imperial Palace in Nara to Kawaguchi Road, but Saga's mighty army blocked their path, leaving them with little choice but to retreat.

It was then that Kusuko and Heizei parted ways. Alone in a roadside hut in the village of Soekami in Koseta, Kusuko swallowed poison and died. Her death was untimely, to be sure, but nonetheless a fitting one for an expert herbalist such as herself. Centuries later, scholars would speculate that it was monkshood—aconite—that Kusuko took to commit suicide, but no one can say for certain.

Prior to that tragic struggle, Prince Takaoka was heir presumptive to the throne. As a result of the uprising, however, it was immediately clear to all that he would never be emperor. It made no difference that Heizei took the tonsure—the Prince was still the son of the instigator. The whole capital sympathized with Takaoka, but for a ten-year-old like him such political matters meant little. Instead, what left a giant hole in the Prince's heart was Kusuko's vanishing like a comet, and taking that sweet image of Hindustan with her.

When the Prince reached his twenties, without warning he shaved his head and renounced the world. It was a decision that could probably be traced back to the vision of Hindustan that Kusuko had instilled in him when he was a boy.

Of course, some prefer the more sober view that the Kusuko Incident represented the beginning of the Prince's increasing frustration with the political world, and this frustration drove him to pursue Buddhism, as similarly desperate conditions had driven the Prince's nephew, Ariwara no Narihira, down the path of erotic pursuits. Yet this banal interpretation cannot adequately account for the rather unconventional Buddhist views that the Prince held throughout his life. For him, the entirety of Buddhism converged on a single point—namely, Hindustan.

There can be no doubt that the Prince was a practitioner of exoticism, in the original sense of the word. That is, he had a deep interest in all things foreign. As an import from the continent, Buddhism had been valued, even vaunted, in Japan since the Asuka period. A great many Buddhists were drawn to the exotic aura of the practice, but for the Prince, Buddhism was this and this alone. It was like an onion—layer after layer of the exotic, with Hindustan at its core.

The great Kūkai was an aesthete and a Hinduphile in his

own right, and so a strong connection between these two pre-eminent Buddhists should hardly surprise us. Kūkai opened his Abhiṣeka Hall on the temple grounds of Tōdaiji in the year Kōnin 13, fifteen years after returning home from Tang. The Prince, who was then twenty-two, wasted no time in befriending the Shingon trailblazer. Indeed, it was in that very hall that the Prince performed the Mandala of the Two Realms and received the title of Ācārya. In the years that followed, the Prince became known as one of Kūkai's most esteemed pupils. When his master passed away, Takaoka was one of the six elite disciples chosen to attend the forty-ninth-day rites and accompany Kūkai's remains to the newly built Oku-no-in on Mount Kōya. He was then thirty-five.

I have no intention of writing an exhaustive biography of the Prince's life here, so I will skip over some of the details. Nonetheless, a few additional events in his earlier years merit our attention. For one, there was the part he played in the restoration of the Great Buddha at Tōdaiji. The Buddha's head had fallen to the ground in the fifth month of the year Saikō 2. The Prince and Fujiwara no Yoshimi were put in charge of its restoration. All together, it took seven years to complete the task; the Buddha's eye-opening ceremony, a lavish event beyond all description, was finally held during the third month of the year Jōgan 3. In that year, the Prince turned sixty-one.

Takaoka traveled to numerous temples near and far. In addition to his staying at Tōji in the capital, there are tales of his journeys to other locales: Yamashina and Daigo Ogurusu to the east; Saihōji to the west; Kongōin in East Maizuru to the north. Although Saihōji would later convert to Rinzai, it belonged to the Shingon sect until the Kamakura period. For a time, the Prince was also in charge of the gigantic Chōshōji in the village of Saki in Nara, near his father's final resting place. From there, the Prince frequently climbed Mount Kōya, the most sacred peak in Shingon Buddhism. There are also indications of pilgrimages he made to Shingon temples throughout South Kawachi and South Yamato.

The Prince's distaste for the banalities of everyday life and his fondness for seclusion earned him the soubriquet "Prince Dhūta." The Prince, whose real name was Takaoka, would come to be known by a variety of nicknames: While later generations would know him by his religious name, Shinnyo Shinnō, he was also known as Prince Zen, the Zen Prince, and the Fallen Prince of the Buddhist Path. The Prince had received stranger names as well, including the Pill-Bug Prince. This curious title appears to refer to the Prince's tendency to turn inward and reflect. Yet this was the very tendency that made the Prince the greatest exote of old Japan.

As we go about retracing Prince Takaoka's footsteps, there is one more event we cannot afford to overlook. The very same month as the eye-opening ceremony marking the completion of the Great Buddha's restoration, the Prince sought permission to embark on a pilgrimage around Japan. The Prince's request appears in the records as follows: "After more than forty years as a priest, I have little life left. Before I die, I wish to see the mountains and the woods. I wish to witness the profundity of the great holy sites." These words strike our hearts even today. According to the same petition, the Prince's entourage would have included five monks, three apprentices, and ten youths. They would have traveled to the western extremes of Japan's main island—the San'in and San'yō regions—and neighboring islands as well. But this pilgrimage never came to pass. And why is that? Although the Prince had asked to travel within Japan, he knew deep down that such a journey could never satisfy him. So, that same month, he submitted a second petition. This time, he sought imperial consent to leave Japan and enter the Tang empire.

On the ninth day of the eighth month of the year Jōgan 3, only five months after the Great Buddha's eyes had been reopened, the Prince presented himself to the Kōrokan authorities in Dazaifu. As soon as things were set in motion, he appeared to forget all about his earlier plans to travel around Japan—his heart was now set on entering Tang. In the seventh month of Jōgan 4, the ship that he had ordered from the Tang merchant Zhang Youxin was ready to sail. Almost immediately, the Prince led a group of sixty—monks and laymen alike— aboard the new vessel and set out for Tang. One of the sixty on that ship was Anten, the monk who would later accompany the Prince on his journey.

The ship waited near Tōchika Island for favorable winds and then sped across the East China Sea, arriving at the port of Mingzhou on the seventh day of the ninth month. From there, the travelers made their way to Yuezhou, where they waited a year and eight months for permission to enter the Tang capital. At last, on the twenty-first day of the fifth month of Jōgan 6, they were granted access, at which point the Prince entered Chang'an from Luoyang. By then, most of the Prince's companions had been allowed to return home. According to the "Brief Record of Prince Dhūta's Entry into the Tang Empire," Emperor Yizong learned from Ensai, a Japanese monk residing in Chang'an at the time, that the Prince had successfully entered the capital, and he was greatly impressed.

Without stopping to rest, the Prince, who had entered Chang'an in the fifth month, had already begun making the necessary arrangements to journey to Hindustan by summer or fall of the same year. Considering this, it seems reasonable to assume that the Prince had been intending to travel to Hindustan all along, and his initial pilgrimage within Japan and even his entry into Chang'an were no more than opening moves toward that end.

Could it really be that the Prince met with the high priests in Luoyang and Chang'an and only then concluded that he would have to travel to Hindustan to pursue the Buddhist Law further? It doesn't seem likely. The Prince got to work as soon as he entered the capital. He immediately set about making the connections that would allow him to begin the final leg of his true journey.

It was in the middle of the tenth month of the same year that, with the permission of the Tang Emperor, the Prince embarked from Chang'an in the highest spirits, following the quickest possible route to the port of Guangzhou. According to the historian Sugimoto Naojirō, who documented the trip in considerable detail, "The Prince headed south from the capital, crossed Mount Zhongnan, and then exited into the Han River Basin. Next, he advanced to Xiangyang, from which point he would have taken either the Qianzhou Mountain Pass or the road to Chenzhou." In either case, four or five thousand li separate Chang'an and Guangzhou, so the Prince and his companions must have spent approximately two months on horseback. No doubt Anten and Engaku were both with the Prince by this time.

The group's arrival in Guangzhou coincided perfectly with the last winds of the northeast monsoon, so the travelers hurried to board a southbound ship. That was on the twenty-seventh day of the first month of Jōgan 7.

ONCE THE SHIP HAD passed between the Leizhou Peninsula and Hainan Island, the Prince and the others noticed that the water below was blue-black and as sticky as birdlime. There was no sign of the anticipated monsoon. In fact, the ship was barely moving. Thick mist shrouded the vessel like a curtain of vapor. Making matters worse, it was stiflingly hot. At night, however, small patches of light that looked like fireflies would appear on the water: *Noctiluca scintillans*—also known as sea sparkles. Although quite common in the area, the sea sparkles provided all on board with some much-needed moments of relief; if not for them, the boredom might have been unbearable.

To relieve the boredom, the Prince sat on the deck and started playing the flute he had acquired in Chang'an. He hadn't expected much from the instrument, but it had a surprisingly fine tone. Notes poured from it, floating out over the water like smoke. Before long, a spot on the water's surface began to bubble and a round head suddenly appeared above the waves, as if summoned by the music. The Prince didn't notice it at first, but Anten did. He asked the shipmaster what it was, and he explained:

"That's a dugong. They're far from rare in these parts."

Desperate for some kind of distraction, the shipmates hoisted the peach-colored creature onto the deck, whereupon the shipmaster fed it cinnamon rice cakes and wine. Apparently sated, it began to doze off. Soon, drops of dung that looked like iridescent bubbles began to slip out of the dugong's rear end.

The bubbles floated into the air, then vanished with a pop.

Akimaru seemed particularly smitten. Timidly, he asked the Prince whether they might keep the creature on the ship if he promised to look after it. The Prince laughed and gave his consent. From that day on, the dugong ate and slept with the rest of the crew.

One day, Anten watched from the shadows as Akimaru played with the dugong. The boy looked intent. He was facing the dugong, speaking to it. Of course, the creature could only wave its flippers in response, but it appeared that Akimaru was trying to get his new pet to talk. Akimaru broke up his words as he spoke, enunciating as carefully as he could:

"Sov . . . ajemto . . . nhi."

Anten was on the verge of laughing, so he turned away. There he saw Engaku, who asked:

"That's not Tang. Is it some tribal language he's speaking?"

In a low voice, Anten answered:

"Yes, I picked up on that too. I believe it's Wuman."

"Wuman . . ."

"Spoken by the Lolo of Inner Yunnan. You know, Akimaru's face is flat and round, not unlike the Lolo . . ."

Before ten days had passed, the dugong was speaking something that sounded vaguely like human language, if fragmentary and imitative, all thanks to Akimaru's dedicated instruction. Its words were of course unintelligible to all except Akimaru. Still, a creature learning to speak is surely something special. Reckoning that this augured well, the Prince was pleased.

It was right around this time that the wind began to blow with fury. The ship was suddenly sailing over the water with incredible speed. Once the wind picked up, it roared continuously, all day and all night. The small vessel was out of control; the crew could do nothing but watch helplessly as the wind drove the craft farther and farther south. No doubt they had sailed well beyond Jiaozhou. It was a blessing that the ship didn't capsize. The crew stayed below deck, hunkered down and praying for land—any land—to come into view. The Prince and everyone else on board became seasick; only Akimaru and the dugong remained curiously unaffected.

At last, the wind died down again. After a good ten days moving south, they finally caught sight of sky through a break in the clouds. Then the lookout yelled at the top of his lungs:

"Land ho!"

These two words filled the crew with new life; they ran to the gunwales to see the reflection of the mountain island floating in the water before them. No, this was no mountain island—it was a jungle coast that ran along the horizon as far as the eye could see.

"Where are we? I imagine we've traveled a good deal south of Jiaozhou."

"I doubt we're anywhere near Jiaozhou now. This is most likely Nhật Nam, the place they call Champa, home of the Viets. Well, well . . . it seems the powerful wind has carried us to some far-flung land!"

"I suppose the name Champa relates to the champak tree that appears in the *Vimalakirti Sutra*, among other texts. Apparently, its flowers are extremely fragrant, drawing garuḍa birds to them from miles away. The tree is known as campaka in Sanskrit."

"Ah, Engaku. You truly are well versed in the sutras. There must be many gold-flowered campaka trees here. Look here, see these? I have no idea what they're called, but their roots reach all the way to the water's edge. Ah, we've landed!"

The ship approached the coiling mangroves, practically running aground. Everyone on board took in the heady, luxuriant smell of plant life for the first time in weeks—it was as if they had been revived. Land at last! Even the dugong waddled off the ship, eager to accompany the others ashore.

A faint trail appeared to lead into the thick jungle. The

Prince and his companions followed it as best they could, cutting through the giant ferns and tangled roots that obstructed their path. Eventually, a vista opened up before them: a field of dead grass, and in the field was a group of men.

They had to be Viet—four or five men sitting in a circle, talking and eating. As the Prince and the others approached, they could see that the men were eating fish and meat with their hands; every now and then, they would dip a straw into a bowl of liquid and snort from it. Each of them did this in turn. Seeing this from a distance, the Prince was unable to contain his curiosity. In a low voice, he said to Engaku:

"Those men are doing something strange. What do you make of it?"

"I've never seen it with my own eyes before, but I imagine this is the famous local custom of nose-drinking. For the Viets, drinking water through the nose holds an indescribable charm."

Just then, the Prince broke wind. The Viet men heard it from where they sat. They stopped their nose-drinking, looked over, and began to shout in an incomprehensible language. Even Anten, who fancied himself quite the polyglot, was not familiar enough with the language to engage them. There was nothing that he or Engaku could do but stand there.

The Viets, however, cast not as much as a glance at Anten, Engaku, or the Prince. Their eyes were fixed on young Akimaru alone. Then, all of a sudden, one of the men reached for the child, grabbed him, and ran off. Akimaru struggled to break free, but his captor was a giant, easily twice his size. No matter how Akimaru flailed about, the man didn't even flinch. Of course, the other travelers could hardly stand by and watch as the man made off with one of their own. Anten was the first to give chase.

When he was younger, Anten was constantly getting into fights. He had once even been expelled from a temple. With supreme confidence in his physical strength, he swept the legs of the giant man out from under him; the Viet fell to his knees and dropped Akimaru with a thud. Anten then head-butted his opponent square in the chest, sending the giant flat onto his back. The monk moved with such speed that the other men had no time to intervene. Stunned, they staggered away in retreat. There was no way to know if they would be returning, but they were gone—at least for the moment.

Akimaru lay unconscious on the grass. The Prince was the first to arrive at the child's side, where he saw something he wasn't supposed to see: Akimaru's clothing had been ripped open from shoulder to chest, exposing a pair of breasts. They were not fully grown, but they were unmistakably the breasts of a young woman.

That night, the travelers set up camp in a clearing in the jungle. Sitting by the fire, the Prince, Anten, and Engaku put their heads together to discuss this development.

"What do you make of three Buddhist monks taking a woman on a voyage to Hindustan? I know how it sounds, but now that we know Akimaru is female, we have no choice but to ask her to find her own way."

"I had a feeling Akimaru's presence might be a hindrance. As we make our way from Yunnan to Hindustan, dangers abound. I seriously doubt a woman's fragile feet could withstand the trek anyway . . ."

The Prince listened in silence as the others shared their opinions. When they were finished, he said with a smile:

"No, there's nothing to worry about. Man or woman, what's the difference? We knew Akimaru to be a young man at first. He only became a woman once we set foot in this land. Who's to say she won't return to being a man as we come closer to our destination? If we can't cope with such minor miracles, I truly doubt we'll ever be able to make it all the way to Hindustan. Whatever the case, it's no trouble for us to take Akimaru as far as she can go."

What the Prince said made no sense to either of his companions, but he had spoken with enough force to put the matter to rest. Anten and Engaku felt ashamed for having given so much thought to such a trivial matter.

At first, the travelers could handle the heat, but after spending the night in the jungle, it began to take its toll. It was unlike anything in Japan—as the high noon rays beat down on the Prince and the others, walking on without shade became unbearable. To lessen their distress, the travelers made straw hats to protect themselves from the sun.

Akimaru made a second hat for the dugong to wear, as if being out of water wasn't painful enough for the sea creature. While the dugong managed to keep pace with the others for some time, the heat ultimately proved too much. Completely drained by the merciless sun, the dugong died that afternoon. Moments before dying, the dugong looked to Akimaru and said in clear language that anyone could understand:

"What a joy this has been. I couldn't say so until it was time for me to die. But I will die with words on my lips. Even when I go, my soul will not vanish. We'll meet again soon—somewhere on the South Sea."

With those words, the dugong shut its eyes. The others dug a hole in a corner of the jungle and carefully lowered the dugong's body into it. The three monks dutifully chanted the sutras. Then the Prince remembered the flute he had been playing when the dugong first appeared. He had an idea—he would play the instrument now, in the dugong's memory. The notes flowed out as if from a fountain, cutting coolly through the jungle.

Just then, a strange beast appeared, shouting:

"What a racket! What a racket! Is that a flute? I was having such a pleasant nap until I was disturbed by that damned flute. Unbelievable!"

The creature was darting all over the place—but what kind of animal was it? Its mouth was elongated like some kind of pipe; its tail was bushy and spread out like a fan; its legs were fluffy as if clad in straw gaiters or fur boots. The animal flicked its tongue repeatedly. As it moved, its tail swept across the ground, sending clouds of dust into the air.

The Prince returned his flute to its brocade bag. Flabbergasted, he turned to Engaku:

"Engaku, you must know. What is the name of this odd-looking creature?"

"I have no idea. There's nothing like it in *The Classic of Mountain and Sea*. It simply defies description. But from what we've seen, it seems to have a command of human language, so I'll ask it a few questions to shed some light on things."

Engaku stepped toward the creature and glared at it.

"Lo, ignorant beast, you dare call the Prince's flute-playing a racket? Such insolence! Perhaps you are unaware, so I shall inform you: This is Prince Shinnyo, third son of Emperor Heizei. Years ago, he left the courtly world and has since attained the title of Master Sage-Priest of the Dharma Lamp. If they have a name for you, tell us now, in good grace!"

The creature seemed unruffled.

"I am a great anteater."

At this, Engaku began to redden with anger.

"Come now, be serious! There are no great anteaters in these climes. It simply isn't possible."

Engaku looked so bellicose that the Prince had to interject:

"Now, now, Engaku. There's no need to lose our tempers. Why should an anteater's presence here bother us any?"

"Miko, you know nothing! That's why you can say such foolish things. At risk of anachronism, let me explain. The great anteater will be discovered roughly six hundred years from now, when Columbus arrives in what will then be called the New World. So how can we be staring at one here and now? Can't you see its very existence defies the laws of time and space? Think about it, Miko!"

The anteater thrust its snout between the two men.

"Wrong, wrong! It's foolish to think that the existence of my kind hinges upon being 'discovered,' as you put it, by Columbus or by any other man. Don't underestimate us! My kind has lived on this planet longer than yours. We can make our home wherever there are ants. To restrict us to the New World—doesn't that smack of anthropocentrism?"

Unflinching, Engaku responded:

"Alright, then. Tell me: When and how did you arrive here from the New World? Answer me this, or I shall have to consider your existence a flat-out falsehood."

"The Amazon River Basin, the birthplace of my kind, is on the exact opposite side of the planet from where we stand now."

"Meaning?"

"Meaning that we are the antipodes of the great anteaters of the New World."

"Pardon? *Antipodes*?"

"Yes. You see, on the other side of the planet are animals that look like us, living upside-down, opposite our feet, almost like a reflection in water. These are our antipodes, and we are theirs. One need not ask if it was them or us that came first. We break down anthills to search for ants to eat, just as they do in the New World. Look around and you'll find no shortage of ant-hills here. The abundance of ants guarantees our right to live here."

Now the Prince cut into the conversation:

"Enough. I'll settle this matter. There is surely some logic to what the great anteater says. Engaku, don't get your back up. Antipodes, eh? You might say we're on our way to Hindustan to see these antipodes of which you speak. Thus, in my eyes, encountering an anteater such as you here is no less than a sign. You mentioned anthills a moment ago, but I have yet to see one. O noble anteater, would you mind showing us one of these hills? And while we're at it, I would love to watch you feast, if it's not an imposition."

At this, the anteater became quite amenable and agreed to lead the travelers into the jungle. Akimaru, ever the animal lover, followed right behind the anteater as they marched toward the largest anthill in the area.

After about a li, the jungle opened up, and there it was. All eyes were riveted on the towering mass. None had ever seen so strange a thing. It looked like a giant pine cone rising from the earth. How could this massive structure have been built by mere insects? It was more like the ruins of an ancient civilization.

The Prince happened to notice a round object embedded in the anthill—but what was it? It appeared to be a glowing green stone, about the size of a peach, lodged just high enough that a person could reach up and grab it. The Prince was fix-ated on the stone. He had to ask the anteater about it. Their host had just clawed a hole into the hill and was extracting a meal of ants with his long tongue, but being questioned by the Prince, he turned to answer:

"According to the lore of our kind, this stone came from across the sea a very long time ago. They say it flew through the air and landed here, where it has remained ever since. There seems to be no way to wrest it free. On nights when the moon shines brightest, the stone, apparently jade, glows green. Moreover, when it lights up, you can see the outline of a bird inside, waiting to be hatched. It seems that the bird in the stone has grown larger with time, nourished by the moonlight. Legend has it that someday the bird will break free from its stone shell, but, when that bird spreads its wings and flies off, my kind will perish. I know how it sounds, but that's legends for you."

Though stoic in mien, the Prince was deeply moved by this. He turned to Engaku and asked nonchalantly:

"When is the next full moon?"

"The gibbous moon is waxing. Should only be a couple of days, I suppose."

On the night of the full moon, the Prince made sure the others were asleep, then left camp and made his way through the jungle. The moon was still rising when he arrived at the dark and imposing anthill, which looked even stranger now than it had in the light of day.

The Prince waited anxiously. After about half an hour, when the moon sat in the very middle of the sky above him, he saw the stone in the hill begin to glow. No, it didn't just glow— the stone grew so blindingly bright that it was impossible for him to turn away. There really was a bird inside, bathing in the brilliant light. It looked as though the bird might break out of the stone at any moment.

Just then, the Prince had a thought. He didn't really believe it himself, but part of him wondered if throwing that stone back toward Japan before the bird broke loose might make time run backward, causing the past to reappear before his eyes. Yes, it was a ridiculous idea. . . . The Prince was thinking about Kusuko, no doubt.

Away, away you go! Off to distant Hindustan!—Kusuko's words played in the Prince's ear like music.

He had to fight temptation. While part of him wanted to see the bird escape its stone egg, another part of him wanted nothing more than to experience the sweet past once again. There was a chance he could be reunited with his beloved Kusuko, and, ultimately, that temptation proved too great. He reached up to grab the bright stone buried in the wall of the anthill. The Prince pulled at it with all his might and . . . the stone came loose! But it tumbled to the ground, whereupon the light inside it vanished. It was instantly reduced to an ordinary rock.

That night, the Prince returned to camp in the lowest of spirits. He kept to himself what had happened at the anthill. Later on, however, when he casually mentioned the anteater in conversation, everyone—Anten, Engaku, and Akimaru— looked at him blankly, as if they had no idea what he was talking about. But how could that be? It seemed the others had never encountered such a creature.

# ORCHID CHAMBERS

*I*n the Yuan dynasty, there was a man named Zhou Daguan who was sent to Chenla for a year as part of an imperial mission; upon his return, he composed *The Gazetteer of Chenla*. According to this text, dozens of harbors dot the Chenla coast, "and all but one of them is shallow and full of silt, making it impossible for larger ships to enter. In these ports, you'll find naught but vines and trees, sand and reeds. Even the most skilled sailors struggle to navigate them."

Prince Takaoka arrived in Chenla some four centuries before Zhou wrote about it, but conditions were similar in his time. As the travelers made their way through the wild reeds of the Mekong Delta, they felt as if they were lost in a maze. Luckily, it was the rainy season and the water was high, so it was easy enough to travel upstream. The Prince and his retinue sailed north for ten days, at which point they learned that they had already pushed well into the continent. There they came upon an enormous lake. In his *Gazetteer*, Zhou would call this place "The Freshwater Sea"; in the local language, it was known as Tonle Sap.

"Never have I seen a lake like this. It must be many times larger than Lake Ōmi."

"Ōmi? Even Dongting pales in comparison! This lake must be swollen well beyond its usual size with rainwater."

Anten and Engaku looked out over the gunwale in awe—silver water as far as the eye could see. In the distance, the lake seemed to merge with the sky. There were no mountains, no trees anywhere. Only water. Being so far south, one might expect to see flocks of birds flying overhead or schools of fish swimming below, but no signs of life were to be found anywhere. Finally, young Akimaru couldn't help but ask:

"Miko, you said we must cross mountains to reach Hindustan, yet I still see none."

The Prince laughed at this.

"You're in for a big surprise if you think we'll reach Hindustan so easily, Akimaru. We won't arrive at the mountains until we've gone a good way north. First comes water. After that, we'll come to the mountains. We have to learn to swim before we can walk."

Just then, the ship came upon a stand of floating wild rice. The shipmaster suggested mooring for a short while, and the Prince consented. The ship would stay there until water and provisions had been replenished.

From the ship, the strip of land looked uncertain, as if it were floating upon the water. Yet when the travelers set foot on the isle, they discovered it was surprisingly solid. Moreover, the stretch of firm ground seemed to continue for some distance. Perhaps it would make for a nice long walk.

With this in mind, the Prince decided to go for a stroll and took Akimaru along. Once they had walked so far that the ship was no larger than a dot in the distance, they found a pool that held some monstrously large fish—"grass-fish," as they were known in Tang. They set about catching the fish with lengths of cane they found nearby, using bits of leaves and stems as bait, and were absorbed in sport when a small boat silently approached. They heard a man's voice:

"What are you doing over there?"

The Prince looked up and found a small man with a yellow, wrinkled face. Rowing with a single oar, he was alone in his boat. He appeared to be advanced in years but was actually much younger than our Prince. What caught the Prince's eye, however, was the man's flamboyant finery: his headgear and green silk robes. They seemed wholly out of place in an area so remote. The Prince looked the man straight in the eye and answered:

"Doing? Can't you tell? We're fishing."

To this, the man replied:

"Ha! From the way you speak, I'm guessing you're not Tang."

"Quite right. As it happens, I'm from Japan."

"Japan! So that makes you Japanese, no? Incredible! I've never met anyone from Japan before. There are so many things I'd like to ask you. Please, come aboard! You too, young man . . ."

Akimaru's hair and dress were not the least bit feminine, so the stranger mistook her for a boy. The Prince motioned toward the vessel moored in the distance and explained:

"That won't do. My companions are waiting for me aboard our ship there. I'm in no position to run off without informing them."

"Come now, it will only take a moment or two. I have something very interesting to show you. A once-in-a-lifetime opportunity, really. Miss it today and you will likely never have another chance."

"Miss what, exactly?"

"The famed harem of Jayavarman the First. There's a channel just ahead that leads to a man-made lake not a li from here. In the middle of this lake sits the island on which we shall find our destination."

The Prince was hardly an expert in Chenla history, so nothing came to mind at the mention of the name Jayavarman. Rather, the Prince simply thought: If Jayavarman happens to be a Buddhist devotee in possession of some knowledge regarding the Holy Land, then taking a moment to visit his so-called harem can hardly be a waste of time. The man continued, almost as though he had read the Prince's mind:

"For ages, kings have attempted to unify the realm of

Chenla, but only Jayavarman the First has succeeded in this task. He's regarded as a chakravartin and worshipped as an incarnation of Maheśvara. Today happens to be the Great King's eightieth birthday, and as part of the celebration his harem will be opened to the public. Even so, that doesn't mean just anyone will be allowed inside. To qualify, one must have standing in the court, as I do. Moreover, even someone with the proper qualifications must present a sanctioned token to gain entry. I happen to have a few in my possession and could have you admitted as my guests. Come, hop in. Let's not waste any more time or we'll be late."

Akimaru tried to signal the Prince with her eyes. She wanted him to refuse the strange man's offer, but the Prince was torn. While he knew that Anten and Engaku would worry, and it was probably best to reject the man's invitation, the Prince could not suppress his curiosity. Finally, he climbed aboard. With great reluctance, Akimaru followed the Prince into the small boat, which could barely hold the three of them. As soon as his passengers had settled in, the man resumed his skillful rowing, sending the small boat gliding across the water.

Once in motion, the man stuck a hand into a cloth sack and pulled out a handful of seashells. He smiled and said:

"Behold. These shells will allow us to enter the harem. I am Tang, born in Wenzhou. So, like you, I am a foreigner in this realm, but I was specially granted these tokens for my years of service in the court."

He then winked at the Prince. The shells he held in his hand were all the same kind of Triton's trumpet.

Soon the boat slid into the channel that the man had mentioned earlier. Or was this more of a canal? The Prince recalled his time in Tang. He remembered taking the Jiangnan Canal north from Hangzhou to Puguangwang Temple in Sizhou with Anten and a number of other attendants. Of course, this waterway was nowhere near as wide. If anything, it bore a greater resemblance to the stone-lined waterways of Hangzhou or Suzhou. At the same time, there were no houses or inns on the banks, nor were there any willows hanging over the water. Indeed, the entire landscape appeared untouched by human hands. The Prince saw no life nearby except for the plants spreading unchecked over the ground and the moss filling the spaces between the stones, which seemed to be crumbling in places. One might reasonably think this whole realm had been abandoned centuries ago. If—what was his name again?—Jaya-varman the First had built this channel, then why? Why here of all places? Something seemed off. This waterway struck the Prince as the very definition of folly.

As they proceeded forward, the plants on the banks, which had been sparse at first, appeared to grow thicker and wilder. There were palms, arecas, banyans—an abundance of aerial roots and strangely twisting tendrils. The Tang man was now rowing at a frenetic pace, and they had come much farther than the Prince could have imagined possible.

The Prince spotted a solitary lizard resting on a sunlit rock, its back shining gold in the light. It was completely motionless, like an objet d'art. Next came a butterfly, clear as glass, fluttering lazily just above the water. He then saw a parrot perched on a branch so low that he thought he could reach up and touch it. As the small boat drew nearer, the colorful bird screamed in a voice that sounded eerily human. All these oddities were entirely new to the Prince, and unlike anything he had ever witnessed back in Japan. How he had longed to encounter such things!

Yet what most piqued the Prince's curiosity were those

things made not by nature, but by man. Cutting deeper into the jungle, they came upon a stone column with a crude, round face, standing in a clearing behind a growth of wild ferns. The Prince wondered what this strange thing might be. Before long, he realized that there were many more such figures, spaced at regular intervals. Each had a face peering from its trunk. Surely they served some ritual purpose, the Prince thought. Still, he had never seen anything like them, even during his time in Tang.

Unable to contain himself any longer, the Prince asked his guide, who had been rowing in silence:

"What is that statue?"

"Oh, that? A lingam."

"Lingam?"

"I suppose it makes sense that someone from Japan would be unfamiliar with such a thing. The lingam is shaped after the phallus of Maheśvara. That's Maheśvara's face carved on it. Maheśvara is Śiva in Sanskrit, yes? Jayavarman the First is thought to be an incarnation of Śiva; the people believe that the King's soul resides within the lingam."

The Prince had no knowledge or experience of phallicism, but nothing the man said struck him as the least bit odd. The word "heretical" never even crossed his mind. If anything, Śiva's childish face and the third eye in the center of the god's forehead filled the Prince with a strange nostalgia. In fact, it made the Prince break into a wide grin. Look! We must be getting closer now. Rejoice! Soon Hindustan will be within my reach. The Prince wanted to shout it out. His heart was racing, and he felt as though he could barely keep it in his chest. Without thinking, the Prince turned toward Akimaru and said:

"Get a good look, Akimaru. These Southern Lands are so

very different from Tang. The face on that lingam looks a bit like yours, don't you think?"

The Prince almost never joked like this. As he became more ebullient, Akimaru grew more cross. On the verge of tears, she said in a low voice:

"Don't be stupid. This is no time for making fun. We have no idea where this man is taking us. I'm scared. And I know Anten will never let me hear the end of it! I should have stopped you when I had the chance . . ."

"Come now, don't be such a worrywart."

They spoke in whispers, but the boat was so small that the Tang man seemed to hear every word.

"There's no reason to be afraid. I'm no slaver. And even if I were, we're heading to the King's Inner Palace, his royal harem. They have no use for the likes of you. Just relax, boy."

Finding scant consolation in the man's remark, Akimaru turned away.

The channel snaked deeper and deeper into the jungle. As the boat slid forth at an even speed, the water splashed rhythmically against the hull. Still no signs of humanity anywhere—only unending forest. The Prince and Akimaru sat astern. Right in front of them, the man was rowing with everything he had, his back to the bow. With his legs firm, he rocked back and forth furiously. It looked as though his headgear might fly off into the water at any moment, yet somehow it never did. When the Tang man first addressed the Prince, he seemed so curious about Japan and its people, but he hadn't said a word about it since; it was almost as if he had completely forgotten. It was by no means easy to know what was on the man's mind. Still, it was too awkward to sit there facing him in total silence, so the Prince made an effort to spark a conversation.

"I became a monk when I was in my twenties. Ever since, I've lived my life without women. Still, when I was younger, I had a wife, with whom I had three children. My father was the Emperor of Japan, so he must have had relations with any number of women: the Empress, ladies-in-waiting, maidservants. . . . I visited my father's Inner Palace from the time I was a boy, so I imagine I have a pretty good idea of what to expect from this harem."

"I see! From your dignified appearance, I assumed you were no commoner, but the son of an emperor? In that case, I'm all the more inclined to guide you around as best I can. I'm sorry to say I know nothing about Japan's Inner Palace, but the Harem of Chenla offers every imaginable delight. After all, it ranks among the finest pleasure parlors in the world—"

"What?"

"I said it ranks among the finest pleasure parlors . . ."

"Were you not talking about the King's harem?"

"I thought I mentioned this, but today is the King's eightieth birthday, so his harem will be opened to the public."

"That much I heard . . ."

"In other words, today and today alone the public can enjoy the harem in the same manner as the King himself. On this day, the harem is a brothel for the common man."

"You don't say . . ."

The man couldn't help noticing the Prince's troubled look. He seemed to understand that his explanation until now had been somewhat lacking. Raising his voice slightly, the man continued:

"It appears you have some doubts, so allow me to clarify. It was Jayavarman the First who established the world-famous Harem of Chenla. From the time the King was young, he has led a debauched life; by the age of thirty, he no longer found satisfaction with ordinary women, so he sent men into neighboring realms to search for beauties of another kind. You see, according to ancient lore, there is a certain tribe in the mountains between Pyu and Yunnan that is said to produce monotreme women, though only rarely. The King set out to find these women. If you should wonder why these monotreme women aroused the King's desire, it is because the esoteric lovemaking treatises of the Brahmins state that these women possess highly valued physical attributes. I shall stop there and leave the rest to your imagination. Personally, I have never set eyes on a monotreme, let alone shared passions with one. So, much like you, I can only guess what these fleshly advantages might be."

Now the Tang man grinned to reveal his blackened teeth for the first time. He then resumed:

"At any rate, the King's men headed deep into Yunnan territory. After spending ten years searching the secluded mountain hamlets of the Lolo Clan, they finally located a few monotreme women. They were immediately brought to the island harem to become the King's playthings, his so-called Gallery of Orchids—orchids being so rare. Yet, from what I hear, these women are more like rare birds than flowers. The King's collection was small at first, but their numbers doubled within a decade. Soon the King had dozens of monotreme women. I don't see how this could have been achieved without developing some way to breed and keep them—something along the lines of animal husbandry."

The Prince muttered to himself:

"But is such a thing even possible?"

Apparently offended, the man snapped back:

"Possible or impossible, isn't that what we're on our way

to see? Let me tell you, the King's Orchids have long been an obsession of mine. I have prayed that one day I might know the King's good fortune and bed such a woman, and that day is today! At long last, the veil shall be pulled away. My wish is mere moments away from being granted, so please refrain from telling me that the Orchids cannot exist. I don't know about Japan or its Inner Palace, but in Chenla, the Orchids make up a very powerful class among the imperial consorts, such that none may doubt their existence."

As the man said this, the boat exited the channel and entered an enormous lake. It was square and looked to be about a hundred li along its perimeter. At its center was a small rocky island covered in jungle. The Prince thought he could see patches of sun-bleached masonry through the dense foliage. Although it seemed patently obvious, the Prince asked anyway:

"That's the island?"

"That's the island." The Tang man's answer rang back full of confidence.

"All you see before you—this lake, this island—the King had made so he could keep his Orchids here. From here, it's a straight line up the waterway to the palace. In this realm, transport relies heavily upon such waterways. A vast network of channels crisscrosses the land."

Strangely enough, as the Prince listened absent-mindedly, he started feeling drowsier and drowsier, until he could no longer resist the desire to sleep. Maybe it was the rhythm of the man's rowing, or the light dancing on the water, or the way the boat was swaying gently from side to side. Whatever it was, it had a hypnotic effect on him. So, almost as if Sleep were dragging him down, the Prince slipped into a dream.

IN THE DREAM, THE Prince was in another boat, but this one was sculled by a boatman. Inside the tiny vessel, the Prince was sitting knee to knee with Kusuko. For the Prince to be here with Kusuko, he had to be a child of about five or six. But if that were so, where was his father? The Prince had once taken such a boat to Chikubu Island at around that age, but his father had gone with him, while Kusuko had not.

"I wasn't with you that day. I really wanted to go, but I couldn't. Do you know why, Miko?"

"No, why?"

"Well, Chikubu is forbidden to women, isn't it? I had to stay behind. But this time it will be fine. Look here."

When the Prince turned to look at Kusuko, she was giving him an alluring smile. Somehow she'd transformed into a young man, gathering her long hair and putting on a long-sleeved robe. The look truly suited her. She was dashing, with a sensuality beyond description. In no way did she resemble a woman of forty.

This clever disguise would undoubtedly allow Kusuko to slip undetected past the vigilant priests on the island, ever on the lookout for female intruders. Delighted, the Prince broke into a grin.

At the same time, it worried the Prince that his father wasn't with them. Never had the Prince left home alone with Kusuko, let alone gone somewhere so distant from the capital. Because the Prince knew in his young heart that Kusuko and his father were more than lord and servant—he knew that they were lovers—he couldn't help feeling racked with guilt at enjoying this time alone with Kusuko. He had done nothing wrong, but he still felt he had somehow betrayed his father. All the same, truly alone with Kusuko for the first time, the Prince found this trip far from unpleasant. In the boat with Kusuko, who was now dressed as a boy, the Prince was unable to contain his glee.

Chikubu was floating in the distance. The cliffs encircling the island appeared to be wearing a hat of thick green trees. The Prince felt sure he'd seen an island just like this before, but he couldn't quite place it. No, of course he couldn't. He was about six years old then, and he had yet to see any islands at all, except for the various islets of Lake Biwa. How could anyone remember what they were only to see in the years to come?

To the east of the island was a narrow inlet. It was the only place to disembark, since the rest of the island was surrounded by steep cliffs. As they stepped out of the boat, they immediately came upon a stone stairway. Whichever temple or shrine one meant to visit, these stairs were the only way to get there. The Prince and Kusuko climbed them hand in hand. In the dream, the Prince felt something akin to pleasure at being easily able to hop up several steps in a single bound.

At the top of the stairs, the Prince found a vermilion-lacquered corridor facing the lake, next to which stood a three-story pagoda. Now, it makes no difference whether such a pagoda existed on the real Chikubu. All that concerns us at present is the pagoda on the island in the Prince's dream. This three-story pagoda was shingled with cypress bark, and when viewed from below, the curve of the roof was breathtaking. The Prince stared up at it, thoroughly entranced, until Kusuko finally tugged him inside.

It took a moment or two for the Prince's eyes to adjust to the darkness. Once his vision returned, he was faced with a Pure Land panorama running along all four walls. He gasped. When was this scene drawn? The rich paint remained startlingly fresh. Amitābha and countless bodhisattvas filled the bottom of the scene, but what truly caught the Prince's eye was a shapely woman with the body of a bird, hovering in the sky above them. Her wings were clearly not the feathered robes of celestial beings; the wings were a part of her. Once this bird-woman had stolen the Prince's eye, he saw nothing else.

In a whisper, he asked Kusuko:

"What is she?"

He pointed at the winged woman.

"A kalaviṅkā."

"A kalaviṅkā."

"Right. A bird from the paradise of Hindustan. They say she sings the most beautiful song, even before she hatches. See how she has a woman's face but a bird's body?"

"She looks just like you, Kusuko."

"You really think so?"

The Prince was quite right. The kalaviṅkā had a full, gentle face, reminiscent of a Tenpyō-era beauty—not at all unlike Kusuko's.

By the time they left the pagoda, the land had already sunk into absolute darkness. They now stood at the highest point on the island, from which they had a view of the distant lake. No—they should have had a view of the lake, but it was a black and moonless night, so they could only guess exactly where the lake lay.

Just then, the Prince thought he saw a gold-colored bird trace a luminous path across the jet-black surface of the lake, flying slightly above the water. At first, he thought it was a fisherman's fire, but this light moved far too quickly and shone far too brilliantly. Soon, another one flew back across the dark water, coming from the opposite direction. Even after it vanished, a golden trail remained etched in the Prince's eye. Now there were three or four of them, flitting across the lake in what appeared to be a playful dance. They must be kalaviṅkās, he thought. Placing his hand on the trunk of a pine, the Prince leaned over the edge of the cliff to get a better look. He thought he heard Kusuko calling:

"Miko, Miko! Come back . . ."

Or perhaps it wasn't Kusuko's voice at all.

"MIKO, MIKO!"

It was Akimaru's hesitant voice waking the Prince from his nap.

"We've reached the island, please rouse yourself."

The Prince opened his eyes to find the very island he had seen in his dream only moments earlier, the island he was sure he'd seen before. What a strange feeling—to return to the age of five or six in a dream, and yet have so recent an experience appear right in the middle of it. When he got a closer look, the Prince saw that this island bore no real resemblance to Chikubu at all. No rocky cliffs—instead, the island before him was flat and framed in sandstone. The Tang man skillfully steered the boat toward a platform with a reptilian railing and a flight of stairs that descended toward the water.

As he leapt from the wobbly craft, the man turned back and shouted:

"Careful now, the lake is teeming with crocodiles. If you were to fall in, it would certainly be the end of you!"

Sure enough, the Prince looked down into the murky water and saw scores of giant crocodiles crawling over one another, their black heads bobbing up and down. Akimaru shrieked and grabbed hold of the still-sleepy Prince. Now he was wide awake.

The railing around the platform took the shape of a snake

and ended in a fan-shaped finial that resembled the head of a cobra about to strike. The three of them made their way across the platform and onto the island. It seemed that the entire isle formed the garden of the harem. What first captured the Prince's attention were the peacocks—were they tame or wild? Plants festooned the grounds; these too may have been wild. Even on the King's island, there appeared to be no signs of human activity. There was a building hidden behind a thick wall of verdure—was this the harem? It was overrun with vines and gave no impression of being inhabited. Even if this place was intended to hold women in isolation, wouldn't it still require guards or attendants?

As they made their way through the tall ferns to the building's entrance, this question weighed more heavily on the Prince's mind. Perhaps the extreme humidity of the region played some part in this, but the building's sandstone walls and pillars were covered from top to bottom in mosses and lichens, and so was the ground. The aerial roots of banyans crept into the walls, forcing them open with monstrous strength. If anyone had been tending to the harem, why had no attempt been made to keep such invasive plants at bay? What possible reason could there be for letting the place fall into such disarray? The Prince wanted to hurl these nagging questions at the man in front of him, but, as if making up for time lost to idle chat, the man was now walking briskly, never once glancing at his companions. He hurried up the steps.

Akimaru eyed the man dubiously and then whispered to the Prince:

"Miko, what if this man isn't right in the head? I thought it odd from the beginning, but this is just bizarre! How could anyone live on an island so barbarous?"

Intricate etchings of all sorts of animals—elephants, tortoises, garuḍas—ran along the outer wall beside the main stairway, but most were worn down and weathered beyond recognition, like the markings left behind by some long-lost civilization. The Prince looked at the unusual reliefs, the likes of which he had never seen in Japan or in Tang, then he climbed the stairs, catching up with the Tang man at the harem gate, where he was anxiously awaiting admission.

In response to the man's frantic cries, a giant ape appeared from behind the half-opened gate. The ape was bright white, right down to his eyebrows. The man kowtowed before the primate and then offered him a grand salute:

"On this day, His Majesty's eightieth birthday, I, Zhang Borong, appear before you in the hopes of enjoying the King's magnanimity. I would be the happiest soul in the land were I permitted to savor one single drop of the fragrant dew of the King's prized Orchids."

He reached into his sack and produced three miniature conch shells, which he then presented to the ape. As if to introduce the Prince and Akimaru to the ape, the man looked back and said:

"These two are with me."

The ape carefully inspected the conches, studying every line and curve. Then, lifting his head, he glared at the man and grumbled:

"No good. I can't accept these. They don't meet the requirements."

At these words, the Tang man became painfully flustered. His hands shook, and in a faltering voice, he begged:

"But, but why? Please tell me why. Three years ago, I received these conches from the Head of Ceremonies . . ."

"Look here. All three shells wind to the right, do they not?"

"What's so horrible about a conch that winds to the right?"

The ape smiled pityingly at the man and explained:

"Dear sir, there appears to be much you don't know, so listen carefully: Viṣṇu carries in his four hands a chakra wheel, a lotus, a mace, and a conch, yes? This conch must wind to the left. Even small children know this. The left-turning conch is a curiosity that can only be found in the waters between southern Hindustan and Sinhala. It is incredibly rare. Why else would the King use Viṣṇu's śaṅkha as his token? Yet here you stand, completely oblivious to this simple fact. . . . Really, sir."

Mocked by the white ape, the man instantly lost all hope. He collapsed on the stone steps and cradled his head in his hands.

Then Akimaru turned to the Prince and said:

"Miko, I have a left-turning conch. I'll give it to you."

Saying this, Akimaru pulled a necklace from her collar with a single shell at its tip. The Prince was taken aback.

"Come now, Akimaru. Don't tell fibs. Why would you have so rare an item hanging around your neck?"

The ape peered over at Akimaru's shell.

"Hm. Small though it may be, this is unmistakably Viṣṇu's śaṅkha. I have no idea how you came across this shell, but having served as guard of the harem these thirty years, I know Viṣṇu's śaṅkha when I see it."

Then Akimaru said to no one in particular:

"My father gave me this shell. I've always kept it with me, but never thought it would be of service in a moment like this."

At this, the man suddenly shot up from the stairs, his eyes aglow:

"How about a trade? I'll give you a hundred liang in gold dust! Well, what do you say, young man?"

Akimaru turned her back to him.

"I say no. I am giving it to the Prince. I would never sell it to you—never."

The Prince didn't know what to say. He looked at Akimaru, then the man, then Akimaru again.

"Well, I am a devout Buddhist, and I already have a good number of years behind me, so I have no more use for women. Even if I were to meet the King's Orchids, what good would come of it? To be honest, I was never all that interested in the first place. I merely accepted this man's invitation. Akimaru, I truly appreciate your generosity, but perhaps you should let this man have the conch. I really don't care to go inside."

Akimaru was adamant, however.

"Miko, please be honest. I know how badly you want to know what waits inside these walls. No need to hold back on my account. Go ahead and get an eyeful. I'll wait for you here."

No sooner had Akimaru placed the precious conch in the Prince's hand than he was pushed through the gate. As the ape guided him toward the Orchids, he looked back forlornly at Akimaru. She stood at the gate, watching him with tears in her eyes.

Onward into the harem. It was a strangely large space with high ceilings. The Prince was led down a corridor lined with columns. Reliefs were etched into the ceiling and walls, no doubt gilded handsomely in the past, but now only unsightly traces remained. Standing by the walls were statues of gods and monsters, a vacant glow in their bejeweled eyes. Every surface was thick with cobwebs. As the Prince walked down the corridor, clouds of dust filled the air, but he said nothing.

The ape pulled out two gauze hoods and handed one to the Prince.

"There are many mosquitoes here. You'd best put this on before stepping into the Orchid Chambers."

Although the Prince had never heard the term "Orchid Chambers" before, he immediately knew that the ape was referring to the boudoirs of the so-called Orchids.

Following the hooded ape down the winding corridor, the Prince found that every twist and turn only served to reveal a space quieter and less alive than the last. At the same time, each new corridor looked so similar that the Prince was convinced he had walked down the same stretch any number of times. He was beginning to feel anxious. He felt he should never have come this far.

To be curious about a harem, at his age . . . The Prince was embarrassed that Akimaru had apparently seen right through him. Perhaps Akimaru knew what was in the Prince's heart precisely because he was so important to her. Thanks to Akimaru, the Prince had learned a secret that had been buried deep in his heart, a truth of which he himself was unaware. But it was too late for regrets now. All the Prince could do was follow where the ape led.

Presently, the ape stopped in the middle of a corridor, then instructed the Prince:

"You must go alone from here. At the end of this passageway, you will find the Orchid Chambers."

Now on his own, the Prince felt even more anxious. He did as the ape said, following the corridor until it led to an octagonal room—a dead end. There was nowhere to go. In the center of the octagon stood a single seat of stone. Thinking he would rest for a moment and consider his next move, whatever that might be, the Prince sat down and wiped the cold sweat from his brow.

He hadn't noticed at first, but as he glanced around the

room, the Prince realized that the eight walls of the room were in fact doors. In other words, the octagonal room was like the center of a flower, the eight rooms its petals. No, one of the eight portals led back to the corridor, so there were in fact seven chambers. Yes, these doors must lead to the Orchid Chambers. Once the Prince recognized this, he noticed the tiling under- foot, a mosaic of sorts, which radiated outward from the stone seat toward the seven doors. As it occurred to him that these chambers had clearly been constructed with beauty in mind, the Prince's anxiety vanished completely.

The Orchids must be waiting behind these doors. If each Orchid had a chamber of her own, there would be seven of them in all. . . . But how could these women live in a place so neglected? Who was responsible for them? Who fed them? According to the Tang man, today marked the King's eightieth birthday—did he still visit the island and enjoy the Orchids' company? For a time, the Prince remained in the stone seat, pondering these questions. The more he pondered, the more he felt a desire to stand up and push open the chamber doors, to see the Orchids for himself. It was an inexplicably powerful desire, considering the fact that he had spent the last forty years without women.

The Prince finally made up his mind. He rose to his feet and walked toward the doors to the immediate left of the ones through which he had entered and pulled on them. They opened with unexpected ease.

So what did the Prince find inside? Well, it was unmistak- ably a woman, exposed on a bed, unabashedly nude and gaz- ing directly at him—but her lower body was covered in brown feathers and did not appear human. Her almond-shaped eyes were open and unblinking. Her breasts had only started to fill in; her hair was long and black, falling over her skinny shoulders and prominent collarbones; she seemed to have no belly button, and even if she did, it would have been hidden beneath her many feathers. The whole time the Prince stood there, marveling at the woman's body with his eyes wide open, she never moved. It was as if she were dead.

The Prince discovered that he lacked the courage to step inside the room. Instead, he drew the doors shut and proceeded to open those to the neighboring chamber. This room was identical to the first. As the Prince expected, another woman was waiting on this bed, but he was shocked to find that she looked exactly like the last one. She had the same almond eyes, the same breasts, the same hair, the same collarbones. The only difference between the two appeared to be the color of their feathers. The first Orchid's feathers had been light brown, but this one had the olive-green plumage of a bush warbler.

The Prince closed the doors and backed away in shock. Upon opening the third set of doors, he found the same sort of woman inside, except her feathers were gray. In the next room was a woman with light-yellow feathers. The next was fuchsia. The next, indigo. The next, silver. Each was resting in an identical pose on an identical bed, as still as death. He wondered if they were in fact dead, but he hesitated to investigate further. He was a monastic, after all, and it struck him as being all too lewd. The Prince simply looked at each of them from the doorway, without laying so much as a finger on any of them.

After seeing the seven chambers with his own eyes, the Prince felt profound relief—and then a sudden and terrible exhaustion. Once again, he collapsed in the stone seat at the center of the octagonal room. For some time, his head was full of visions of colorful birds with women's faces. The Prince was now so tired that he wanted to surrender to sleep, but he summoned the strength to walk back down the corridor to Akimaru. At the thought that she would be waiting there, the Prince's steps grew lighter and lighter.

ACCORDING TO THE STONE inscriptions that chronicle the lives of the Chenla kings, Jayavarman the First reigned over his kingdom for nearly twenty-five years, from 657 to 681 by the Gregorian calendar. If this is true, the King lived a full two hundred years before the Prince began his voyage to Hindustan. In other words, what the Tang official Zhang Borong had suggested—that the Prince had happened to reach Chenla on the King's eightieth birthday—was out of the realm of possibility. It is unclear exactly where Zhang had gone wrong, but there can be no doubt that the man had committed a serious anachronism.

# GARDEN OF DREAMS

The name Panpan likely first appeared in the Tang-dynasty *History of Liang*. In this volume, we find six nations along the Malay Peninsula: Tenasserim, Bujang, Panpan, Tandang, Kantoli, and Langkasuka. It was in the late sixth and early seventh centuries that Chenla rose to power, threatening Funan, which had long been under the influence of Indian civilization, and pushing Funanese culture and Mahāyāna Buddhism southward into Panpan, which was located around the middle of the peninsula, overlooking the Bay of Bandung. While the nations surrounding it soon fell into obscurity, Panpan alone continued to thrive. It probably owed its survival to its advantageous location between Nālandā—the heart of Mahāyāna learning in eastern India—and the Buddhist kingdom of Srivijaya, which had only recently emerged on the Isle of Sumatra. On the other hand, the profusion of spectacular Buddhist ruins discovered within Panpan has led some to believe that the capital of Srivijaya was not on Sumatra at all, but in Panpan itself. As noted in "The Greater Court Hymns" of *The Book of Odes*, the Governor of Panpan kept a menagerie. For our purposes, we should think of this place as a kind of zoo, where King Wen of Zhou kept all manner of birds and beasts and let them roam freely.

At the end of the seventh century, the Tang monk Yijing traveled to Hindustan in search of the Dharma; on the way, however, he stayed in Srivijaya and the Southern Lands for as long as seven and a half years. We may imagine that he was one of only a few Buddhist travelers to visit Panpan before Prince Takaoka—some two hundred years earlier. Moreover, Yijing was ultimately successful in his journey to Hindustan and, in this regard, surely served as a model for the Prince. Yet we must not assume that Prince Takaoka had much knowledge of Yijing or the route that he took to the west. In fact, he was probably unaware of the very existence of the Buddhist nation that was then flowering along the Malay Peninsula.

IT WAS A TERRIBLY hot day. A thick canopy of wild rubber trees, coconut palms, and banana plants left the path dark even at midday. In the heat, our travelers had forgotten all about their goal of Hindustan. They only wondered what they were doing wandering around a place such as this. It was so hot that they felt they were losing their minds, and—to some degree—they were. The travelers could not even be sure if they were headed toward Hindustan, but they continued to walk on endlessly, blindly. To lift their sinking spirits, the Prince pointed out nearby plants as well as the various insects buzzing around them. He commented on how different the flora and fauna in these parts were from those of his native Japan. Engaku, an expert in matters of botany, then added detailed explanations to the Prince's simple observations:

"This one resembles a plant known as Shell-Mother. Go ahead and pluck it. Its clustered roots look just like little sea-shells—hence the name. I've never seen a specimen with flowers so large."

Akimaru spotted a large pill-bug hiding under a stone, at which Engaku hastened to add:

"This is what we call Ratswife. *The Ready Rectifier* identifies it as Rat's Burden, because of its tendency to attach itself to the backs of burrowing rodents. Nowadays, however, the insect is most commonly known as Ratswife, which fails entirely to convey the nature of its relationship to rats. The stories about rats eating the bugs and becoming unusually amorous are just that: stories. Old wives' tales, so to speak. Go ahead, touch it. It should ball right up."

As the group headed deeper into the jungle, the trees gave way to a meadow with short green grass, sparkling in the sunlight. Right in the middle of the field were a couple of coconut palms. With the sun now beating down on them directly, it should have been even harder to bear, but a breeze was blowing through the clearing. Finding some degree of respite, the travelers paused there for a moment to consider their next steps.

Akimaru crouched down on the grass and let out a shrill cry:

"What a strange thing! Is it a mushroom? Sir Engaku, please tell me. What is this?"

Everyone gathered around to take a close look at the object in question, which appeared to be rooted in the earth. It was whitish and covered in a thin membrane, under which was some sort of foamy substance. It almost appeared to have no solidity at all. Engaku stared at it intently and then announced:

"A fungus resembling this one has gone by the name of Mare's Muck. It's also known as the Giant Puffball. Maybe that's what this is. If so, a light strike will release a puff of smoke from a tiny hole near its top. Shall I try?"

When Engaku touched the thing with his finger, it instantly shrank in upon itself. No puff of dust. It merely rolled away, propelled by the wind. It seemed the object was not, in fact, tethered to the ground. As the ball tumbled off, the air around them filled with an indescribably pleasant fragrance. Now thoroughly intoxicated, the Prince said:

"How curious . . . a fragrance that defies description. Never have I smelled such a thing, and yet it's so familiar. So much so it feels as though it's sinking into my very bones. Engaku, my dear friend, it seems you've missed the mark this time. That was no mushroom."

Engaku nodded and said:

"Quite so, Miko. It probably wasn't even a plant. That fragrance, I daresay, is much more like a woman's powders . . ."

Anten shot a sharp glance at his fellow monk.

"Pardon me, but is your experience of womankind great enough for you to speak so knowledgeably?"

At this, Engaku was at a loss for words.

Meanwhile, Akimaru had chased after the windblown ball, taken it in her hands, and thrust her nose directly into it to take the deepest whiff she could. It seemed she was paying no attention to the others as they spoke. Anten frowned and cautioned the child:

"Akimaru, please temper yourself. It may smell sweet, but that doesn't mean you can lower your guard. We know nothing of this odd object. It may harbor poisons within. Stop toying with it at once!"

Heeding those sharp words, Akimaru finally tossed the thing to the ground, but she had a vacant look in her eyes, as if she couldn't get the sweet-smelling thing out of her mind.

They had all been struck dumb by the curious orb, but without another word they collected themselves and left the field. Back in the jungle, however, they immediately found many more of those balls scattered along the path. What could they be? All were dying to know, but none dared ask aloud.

Before long, Akimaru could no longer restrain herself—she bent down to grab one, picking it up and lifting it to her nose so quickly that no one could intervene. She longed for another dose of that unforgettable ambrosia, but this time was nothing like the first. Akimaru breathed in deeply and then instantly stumbled to the ground, her face sapped of all color.

"Idiot, what did I tell you?"

Anten angrily kicked away the ball at his feet, but by then the unbearably foul stench had entered the nostrils of all present. Akimaru, who was down on all fours, crying and vomiting uncontrollably, was worst hit. The Prince patted her on the back and said:

"They look alike, no doubt. Still, one gave off the most intoxicating fragrance imaginable, the other a stench so terrible it makes you sick to your stomach. Knowing as little as we do, we'd better keep our wits about us. Best not to act impetuously from now on. Clearly, there are things in these parts that leave even our most knowledgeable herbalist stumped. In the Southern Lands, we will encounter many mysteries that defy our wildest dreams. Of this we can be certain. Let us be glad this was not so serious, and I am sure Akimaru has learned a valuable lesson. Now, let's press on a little more before the sun sets."

So the Prince rose and the group set off once again. For a time, Akimaru seemed unusually meek. Yet once everything was out of her system, she looked fine, as if nothing had happened.

When they finally reached the jungle's edge, a large valley opened up before their eyes. The sun was setting, filling the valley with shadow. The travelers could nonetheless make out the pointed tops of buildings and several columns of smoke among the thick patches of trees—this had to be a village. Anten stood on the slope with a pensive look, studying the scene below. He spoke:

"It could be dangerous to enter. Engaku and I will go ahead to investigate. Miko, please wait here until we return."

The two monks made their way straight down, leaping from rock to rock, slashing through the bramble and brush in their way. Just as the two of them disappeared from view, an animal appeared from behind a nearby rock. Caught off guard, the Prince froze.

The beast had the appearance of a boar but was much larger, and very round indeed. Its fur was striped black and white, and lustrous like satin. It had narrow eyes like a pig and a wrinkled snout. This snout was the animal's most curious feature. It was long and twisted like a trumpet, its wet tip twitching ceaselessly. The animal was looking at the Prince, but it soon became apparent that the gentle creature posed no threat to them. Akimaru stepped toward the animal, presumably to pet it, but the creature turned the other way, lifted its short tail, and released a single ball from its rear end that fell with a plop.

At this, the Prince howled with laughter. But, as he and Akimaru inspected the droppings, their eyes met. The secret was out! What they had thought to be a mushroom or some kind of plant was in fact excrement! At this realization, the Prince's mind raced. What shocked faces would Anten and Engaku make when he shared this bit of knowledge with them? Akimaru appeared to be thinking something similar as she gave the freshly deposited feces a long look.

Just then, a voice came from behind them:

"Meliya hulay hulay-hu."

The Prince and Akimaru turned around to face the strange voice and were startled to find a line of men standing behind the rocks, looking at them with probing eyes. The half-naked men all had brightly colored feathers on their heads, golden rings dangling from their noses, and straw skirts covering their loins. They appeared to be searching for the animal. One of the men stepped forward and cried:

"Hu-hu, hu-hu!"

At that call, the beast reappeared. Apparently domesticated, it wobbled toward the man beckoning it, who then quickly leashed the animal, tightening a chain around its neck.

The Prince and Akimaru stood there dumbfounded. Then the same man gave some sort of hand signal to the others, at which point a swarm descended upon the travelers, forcing them to the ground and swiftly binding their hands behind their backs. It all happened in the blink of an eye.

The men yelled excitedly, and with a tug on the animal's leash, they set off down the slope, through the undergrowth, prodding the backs of their new captives with sticks. Without the use of their hands, the Prince and Akimaru had no choice but to walk on, slipping and staggering through the mud. There were giant gadflies hovering around the bushes, buzzing in the prisoners' faces, but they could not even shoo the insects away.

At the bottom of the valley, the group waded through the shallows, over which massive vines were hanging, then they continued onto the other bank. Rows of palms lined the path. Before them stood a raised thatched hut—and next to that was an enormous hole dug deep into the reddish earth. The men untied the Prince and Akimaru, then shoved them into the pit. This was to be their prison, it seemed. The men withdrew, leaving behind only the echoes of their mocking laughter.

The Prince sighed and said:

"What gross misfortune that those men set upon us in the absence of Anten and Engaku. Or perhaps they had been watching our every move, waiting for that moment. I'm afraid we've come to a dreadful place."

Dejected, Akimaru added:

"I was wrong to try to pet the animal. Why does my impetuousness always get us into trouble?"

"No, the fault is not yours alone, Akimaru. When you tried

to pet the beast, it faced the other way and defecated. I couldn't keep myself from laughing out loud, and the villagers may well have heard me. We all slip up at some point."

In the morning, as the Prince and Akimaru fed on the bunch of bananas that had been tossed into the pit, they noticed a clamoring crowd gathering near the pit's edge. The person who at last appeared overhead was a dignified character, presumably the village headman or a nobleman of some kind. He had a white sash draped over his shoulder, a sword hanging at his waist, and a beard on his chin. He stood over the pit ominously, a grin stretched across his face. He spoke slowly—in fluent Tang:

"I am the Governor of Panpan, and you are trespassing upon my territory. Tell me right away where it is you mean to go."

The Prince had little difficulty understanding what the man said. Looking up from the bottom of the pit, he replied just as clearly in the same tongue:

"We had no idea that we were trespassing upon your land. We only wish to make our way to Hindustan."

"Hindustan, you say? What do you seek in distant Hindustan?"

For whatever reason, the Prince was unable to answer this seemingly simple question. Wasn't his purpose clear? Wasn't he on a holy journey? Wasn't that why he took the tonsure not long after turning twenty, and why he risked his very life to voyage to Hindustan now, forty years later? So why did he suddenly find himself tongue-tied? Maybe it seemed too obvious to be stated aloud, and he felt somehow embarrassed. Or perhaps he was not entirely sure that what he sought in Hindustan was in fact the Dharma. What first captured his interest was nothing so grand. As a child, he was told many curious stories about the place, and this, it would seem, had more to do with his present voyage than any matter of faith.

After much thought, the Prince's reply was uncharacteristically circuitous. Instead of simply saying, "I am on a holy journey," he went on at length:

"As I was born in the far eastern reaches of the world, Hindustan has long been the land of my dreams. In fact, it was for this reason that I took the tonsure. . . . So it is not that I seek the Dharma, not exactly. For me, the way of the Buddha and the path to Hindustan are one and the same. This is why I have set my heart on this journey."

The Governor laughed heartily.

"Mercy, are all Buddhists from your country so prone to grandiose speech? You ought to know, there's no need to travel as far as Hindustan. Right here and now, in this very land of Panpan, the Light of the Buddha shines all around you. The Buddhadharma is in full, sweet bloom, and if you wish, I can provide ample evidence. Or perhaps it is proof enough that more monks from Chang'an come here to study than go to Hindustan."

The Governor spoke confidently before suddenly changing his tone:

"Let me ask, are you inclined to dream often?"

The Prince was not at all sure what the Governor was driving at—still, he had always been proud of his ability to dream, ever since he was a boy. So, without the slightest hesitation, the Prince responded:

"Yes, I dream often."

This had the Governor beaming.

"What luck. How often, would you say?"

"I rarely if ever sleep a night without dreaming."

"All the better, all the better. Still, there are good dreams and bad dreams. . . . Which would you say you're more likely to have?"

"Well, I doubt I've ever known a bad one. My dreams tend to be entirely pleasant."

Now the Governor was so happy that he was almost moved to tears.

"How wonderful! It seems our patience has been rewarded. Here, in the Southern Lands, the sun beats down on our heads so intensely that its radiance disturbs our thoughts well into the night. So, very few have known the splendor of dreams. A dreamer such as you is, as they say, one in a million. I understand that your heart is set on this voyage to Hindustan, but—if you can dream as well as you say—I must ask: Why put yourself through the trials of travel? Is it not enough to dream of the place nightly? Regardless, I will have you sent to the Garden of Dreams straightaway. Thanks to you, dreamer, the garden just might return to its former glory."

"Garden of Dreams, you say?"

The Prince repeated his words, but the Governor continued unfazed:

"Oh, rest assured, you shall be well cared for there."

Then, acknowledging Akimaru, he asked:

"Who is this child? Your page?"

The Prince nodded.

"So be it. The child shall accompany you to the garden. You will lodge in the same quarters."

With a smile of satisfaction on his face, the Governor backed away from the pit's edge.

The next day, an elephant cart arrived. The Prince and

Akimaru were taken from the pit where they had been held for two days, loaded into the cart, and sent to the so-called Garden of Dreams. Seeing an elephant for the first time in their lives, the two were amazed to discover that there were creatures with trunks even longer than that of the odd animal they had seen defecating on the day they arrived.

Now, what was this Garden of Dreams? It was a part of the legendary menagerie that had been maintained by generations of Panpan rulers. In a clearing in the jungle stood a spacious park with fenced enclosures for tigers and bears, cages for rhinoceroses and other rare beasts, and birdhouses for exotic fowl, many of which were unique to the Malay Peninsula, including white peacocks and sugarbirds, as well as red, green, and indigo parrots.

When Yijing visited Panpan, he too must have come to this very park. So beloved had this tropical paradise been since ancient times that nothing brought the Governor greater pride than preserving it just as his ancestors had done before him.

The place called the Garden of Dreams occupied the very heart of the park. Living in this enclosure were the baku—the type of animal that the Prince and Akimaru had seen two days earlier. As described in ancient texts, this beast possesses the trunk of an elephant, the eyes of a rhinoceros, the tail of a bull, and the paws of a tiger. Yet to the Prince's and Akimaru's eyes, there was nothing particularly fantastic about this creature. It was somewhat grotesque, yes, but it still looked like an ordinary mammal. Belying its unassuming appearance, however, the baku had a taste for luxury. The baku quarters were especially lavish, being built of brick and boasting their own keeper's lodge. It seemed the sensitive animals required an attendant to see to their many needs and demands at all times of day and night.

The Prince and Akimaru arrived at the garden right as the animals were enjoying their afternoon outing on the grass. One of the three appeared to be the recent escapee that had surprised them the other day. Countless orbs were strewn all around. Akimaru pointed at one and sniggered to the Prince. In that moment, the keeper came through the gate and commented:

"Ah, those are the dregs of dreams."

"Dregs, you say."

"Verily. The baku eat nothing but the dreams of men, you know. That being so, looking after them is not without its share of hardship."

The keeper grabbed a broom and a dustpan, then briskly went about sweeping up. This man, certainly an official of some stature, spoke in fluent Tang no less clear than that of the Governor. Holding the collected waste up to his nose, the keeper sniffed cautiously and then made a sour face.

"Putrid, yet again. Sad as it is, the animals have eaten nothing but bad dreams recently. When they feast on fine dreams, their dung gives off the most intoxicating smell. But when the dreams are inferior, nothing can be further from the truth. These poor dream-loving creatures . . . How difficult life must be when there are only unpleasant dreams to eat."

The keeper was muttering to himself, it seemed, but the Prince had to satisfy the curiosity rising within him, so he asked in spite of himself:

"Why is it, if the baku are so difficult, that you keep them here?"

"There's tradition, for one thing. It was six reigns ago that this park was built. In those days, Panpan's territory was vast. The kingdom was at the height of its power. Consequently, it had no trouble supplying the animals with a good stock of dreams. Talented dreamers from the north—the Lolo—flooded into our lands in large numbers for the sole purpose of feeding the dream-eaters delectable visions. But when Chenla took the north of Panpan, the source of our most talented dreamers was suddenly cut off. With that, the garden's upkeep became a greater challenge than we could ever have imagined. This is, of course, because the sun-soaked people of our land are almost entirely without the luxury of dreams. In the golden age, the garden had as many as twenty creatures, but that number has since dwindled to a meager three. And even these three are starved for satisfying dreams, so they flee the premises in search of a decent meal. Why, one of them tried to escape just the other day."

"If it's come to that, why not close the garden entirely?"

The keeper shook his head at the Prince's suggestion.

"Again, tradition. There's the reputation of Panpan to consider, and the present policy of our nation is to preserve the glorious garden exactly as it has existed for generations. This is also My Lord's view of the matter, though he does have his own way of seeing things . . ."

"His own way?"

"Yes. This pertains to the secrets of the Governor's family, so I mustn't speak too loudly. Yet I am certain he would not mind my sharing this with you. For some time now, his dear and only daughter, Princess Phatalia Phatata, has suffered from a melancholy of unknown origin, often sleeping for days at a time. At his wit's end, My Lord turned to a Brahmin, who was of the opinion that the cure could be found in the flesh of the baku. Their flesh, you see, is made of the essence of dreams—hence it has the power to purge the body of any dark influences. Should the baku have their fill of pleasant dreams, the power of their flesh would be that much greater. Any illness would be cured in short order. At any rate, when My Lord heard this, it gave him such hope. You see, all is arranged for the Princess to marry the Prince of Srivijaya, and the Governor believes it is of the utmost importance that his daughter be free of her sickness before her wedding day comes."

"Yet as long as the baku are dropping only the foulest dung, no amount of flesh will rid the Princess of her woes."

"Exactly. We have the most desperate need for a man inclined to dream the finest dreams. So, it seems, you are just what the Brahmin ordered."

"I see."

The Prince, his usual eloquence having deserted him, had nothing else to say.

THE BRICK HOUSE BUILT for the baku was surprisingly spacious. Contained within it was another, smaller building. This building-within-a-building consisted of a single large room in which the dreamer slept. At its center was a stone bed with a strange ceramic pillow. Aside from that, there were no furnishings of any kind. Each wall had a small opening through which the baku could be seen wandering outside, but of course the openings were too small for the animals to pass through. That is, the baku were confined to the ring encircling the room in which the dreamer slept, where they wandered all night in search of dreams.

Apparently, the baku fed from a distance, without ever physically touching the dreamer. It was enough for the animals to probe the small openings with their snouts. The first night that the Prince slept on the dreamer's bed, he felt anxious. Of course, everything was fine—the animals didn't lick his face or anything like that.

When he awoke in the morning to find that the night had passed without incident, he was relieved, but one thing still concerned him. No matter how he tried, the Prince could not remember dreaming during the night. It was as though his mind was perfectly blank, and he said as much to the keeper when they met that day.

"Sadly, I dreamed nothing last night. In my sixty-odd years of life, I have seldom had a night like this. The baku must be sorely disappointed. It seems I've let them down . . ."

The keeper only smiled and said:

"Oh, far from it. You dreamed, all right. Come morning, each of the dream-eaters had dropped the most fragrant dung. It's only that they ate every bit of your dreams, so you haven't even a scrap of memory left. Nothing to worry about."

That explained it. The Prince was convinced by what the keeper said, but he also felt as if something was missing. Since boyhood, the Prince had been a gifted dreamer who could take pride in the pleasantness of his dreams—dreams that seemed all the more pleasant when remembered after the fact. For the Prince, his dreams were memory itself; if he was unable to return to them, then his dreams were as good as dead. What a lifeless way to wake up, always empty-minded, picked clean by the insatiable baku. If he had to live like this—dreaming night after night, but never remembering—what kind of life would that be?

Lying on the stone bed with his head on the pillow, the Prince sank into melancholy. During the day, when he met with Akimaru, he no longer made jokes or laughed as he had before. Akimaru had no idea what to do. She could only gaze with concern at the Prince's forlorn face. Immediately and irrevocably forgetting his dreams even as he dreamt—who could have known this would be so disturbing? The Prince was frustrated beyond belief.

In place of his lost dreams, the Prince began to see strange visions as he slept. These visions could hardly be called dreams—they were more like the detritus of dreams, pale shadows appearing on a night-black screen in his mind. The stripes of light and dark that the Prince thought he saw in his mind led him to suspect that it was the baku that were behind the shadows. What if they had consumed the last of his dreams and moved deeper into his mind looking for more to eat? Sometimes the Prince feared that the animals were devouring his mind. He would wake up screaming in terror. He couldn't shake the horrifying thought that since he had no dreams left, the animals had moved on and were now nibbling on his very brain.

More than ten days had passed when the Prince, keenly aware that his mind and his body were shriveling up, had a now-rare dream—a dream that, for once, stayed with him. No such thing had happened since he came to the so-called Garden of Dreams. Yet this particular dream was not of the pleasant variety that the Prince used to know.

For the first time in his life, the Prince had a genuine, heart-wrenching nightmare, and it went like this:

The setting seemed to be the Sentō Palace in Nara—the Thatched Villa—which belonged to the Prince's father, the former Emperor Heizei. His father was in bed, and appeared to be ill. Next to him, Kusuko had set out an array of large and small plates and bowls, and was grinding herbs: most likely haritakī bark, areca nut, cassia, monkshood, some type of rheum plant, and so on. The place was filled with nothing but the sound of stone against stone.

The Prince, a child of eight or nine at the time, felt as though he was seeing something he shouldn't as he watched the scene unfold from under the eaves.

Suddenly, as if waking from a nightmare, his father sat up and began rambling deliriously.

"The spirit of my father appeared to me in a dream. His brother, Prince Sawara, came to Kashiwabara to beg forgiveness, he says. Still, Sawara was full of regret that his bloodline had to end—it broke his heart."

Her hand still stirring, Kusuko responded:

"You're speaking nonsense, My Lord. Your fever is running high and you're having wicked dreams, that's all. It's the purity in your heart, you know. The evil spirits have their eyes on you. Come now, your medicine is ready, so please, take it and rest."

She spoke as though placating a child.

Kusuko placed the powder and a cup of sake in front of him. He merely stared blankly for a time, but at Kusuko's urging he took the cup in his shaky hands and swallowed the powder along with the drink. With that, Kusuko rose to her feet, held her fan, and started to dance:

> When the merry Miwa
> Opens his gate to bless us
> And the spirits begin to flow
> Merry may he be, merry may we be

Kusuko waved her long sleeves this way and that, singing in a low voice as she swayed. The Prince had never seen her like this before. He knew her to be so straightforward and open; he had always engaged with her as a friend—as a peer. The woman now dancing before his father eluded his understanding. He thought he could detect a sinister half-smile on her face. On the other side of the silk curtain, the anxious Prince cried out under his breath:

"Father, Father . . ."

But the Prince's words didn't reach him. Kusuko continued to dance as if nothing had happened, with the Emperor watching her every move, entranced. Kusuko sang in a voice that was light and easy, but for some reason it had the opposite effect on the young Prince. It weighed heavily his heart.

"Merry may he be, merry may we be."

After her dance, Kusuko returned to the Prince's father and urged him to drink another round of what she'd prepared. He appeared to not want to drink it, but Kusuko wouldn't take no for an answer. Again and again, she pressed him, but he would not lift the cup.

Kusuko looked away in irritation.

In that moment, the Prince's eyes, hidden in the half-light under the eaves, met Kusuko's. Maybe it was nothing, but the Prince thought he saw a cruel twinkle of light. A shudder ran through him, and he shouted out as if he were on fire:

"Stop it! You're killing him . . ."

Kusuko's reply was so cold that, even when he remembered it now, his heart froze. He could only think that Kusuko harbored some secret malice, that she was pretending to mishear what he had said. Perversely, she responded:

"Miko, what's come over you? Why would you ask me to kill your dear father? What a horrible thing to say!"

Then the dream ended, abruptly. The Prince awoke in a cold sweat, but Kusuko's voice still rang in his ears, and the sinister look in her eyes haunted him.

THE KEEPER KNOCKED AT the door to the dreamer's room two or three days later. He reported to the Prince that Princess Phatalia Phatata would visit the Garden of Dreams that afternoon, as had been planned, and ordered him to prepare for her arrival.

The garden had housed three baku until quite recently, but now only one animal remained. The flesh of the others had no doubt been fed to the Princess in the hopes of curing her. What would they do once she had eaten the last one? The Prince could not know, nor was it his place to ask. Yet, according to the keeper, the entire land of Panpan, every official and every citizen, was scouring the nearby hills for more baku.

When the Governor's daughter arrived at the garden dressed in finery and accompanied by her ladies, the Prince doubted his own eyes. She couldn't have been more than thirteen or so, yet she was the spitting image of Kusuko.

Moreover, the cruelty the Prince had never even imagined in Kusuko, until he saw it on her face the other night in his sleep, was evident in this girl—and perhaps even stronger in her. A glint of wickedness. This is not to say her face always appeared that way. Rather, like the sun shining brightly before hiding itself behind a cloud, her beautiful face revealed a certain cruelty only for an instant. It reminded the Prince of how when the dream-eater curved its body its coat would shine, briefly, like velvet.

The Princess, they said, suffered from melancholy—yet there wasn't even a trace of it now, perhaps thanks to the flesh she had eaten.

With an air of familiarity, the girl threw open the door to the enclosure and strode inside. It was hard to imagine that this was her first time visiting the garden. The last remaining baku happened to be strolling across the lawn right then, and when it spotted the girl, it rushed toward her excitedly.

It was likely not the first time these two had met—the animal was visibly comfortable with the Princess. As she stroked its fur, the baku began to display signs of arousal. It got up on its hind legs, rolled on the ground, trumpeted loudly through its trunk, and ran in circles around the girl. The Princess looked back to her ladies and said:

"The baku is by its nature a jealous creature. If you don't fancy being bitten, you had best stay outside the fence. Understood?"

Needing no such warning, the ladies stood fast by the fence, watching with bright eyes every movement their mistress and the animal made.

Where was the Prince standing when this happened? Was he standing on the other side of the fence with the ladies? Or was he with the keeper, looking on from the brick entrance? It was entirely unclear to him. Was this a dream too? He was so unsure of his own place in the scene that he doubted it could be real. Everything seemed out of focus. Only the Princess, an incarnation of Kusuko herself, had a curious vividness about her. Magnified at the center of the Prince's field of vision, she was all he saw.

For whatever reason, the Prince had expected that a girl fed on the flesh of the baku would be fat and greasy—wholly unpleasant to look at. Yet the Princess he saw now completely betrayed that notion. The sight of the girl playing with the baku was thoroughly enchanting, transforming the Prince into nothing but eyes.

Under the fascinated gazes of the women outside the fence, the baku now reached the peak of its excitement, throwing itself belly-up on the grass and pulling its legs close to its body. The animal shut its eyes tight in anticipation of the girl's caresses. Its penis now grew to an absurd length, slapping against its fat belly. With a smile, the girl knelt down and took the animal's penis in one hand, then pressed it lightly against her cheek, nestling it in her long hair. Same as the baku, the girl was clearly aware that she was being watched as she performed this series of intimate acts. Under the attention of all the onlookers, the baku also appeared to experience an even greater pleasure. Once the animal's cries of ecstasy reached a new height, the girl placed its penis in her mouth. Her eyes were still smiling, but the Prince thought he noticed something sinister in her expression.

Curiously enough, as the Prince followed the scene with absolute intensity, he grew convinced that he was, in fact, the dream-eater. He had become the baku receiving the girl's affection. Yes, he remembered when he was a boy of five or six and Kusuko had her hands between his legs. That was the Prince's first experience of the pleasures of the flesh. He recalled it now, and it overlapped with the scene before him. She really did look like Kusuko. Or maybe the Prince identified with the baku so easily because he knew that the animal survived solely on his nightly dreams. The dream-eaters had fed on his dreams, and the girl had fed on their flesh—so it could be said that, through the baku, the Prince and the Princess shared a most intimate connection. Was she not living through his dreams? It occurred to him that she might not even exist were it not for them.

At every playful movement the Princess made, the baku produced a sound like a flute, suggesting its approaching climax. And then the moment was over. Compared to all that had led up to it, the finale was all too brief. The animal convulsed two or three times before collapsing limply. Even the beast looked surprised by what had happened as it turned in a daze toward the onlooking ladies.

But by then the Prince was no longer watching. The instant

the baku ejaculated, everything he saw vanished, and he fell into a world of perfect darkness—was this dream or reality?

"Please wake up, Miko. Anten and Engaku have returned with wonderful news. The land of Panpan, just beyond the valley, is preparing for your arrival."

As Akimaru whispered these words in the Prince's ear, he opened his eyes and said with a smile on his lips:

"Panpan? Why, I was just there."

# HONEY MAN

The Governor of Panpan was a devout Buddhist and a generous man. When he heard that the Prince's desire to travel to Hindustan hadn't wavered, he was so moved that he prepared a ship specifically for him and his companions: an Arab-style vessel with sails hoisted by capstans. The travelers left from Takkola, an old seaport on the western coast of the Malay Peninsula that makes an appearance in Ptolemy's mid-second-century *Geographia*. The Governor and his retainers had seen them off, and their vessel was now headed toward the Bay of Bengal. Assuming they were blessed with favorable winds, they would soon arrive near the mouth of the Ganges. They were bound for Tamralipti, another ancient port that can be found on Ptolemy's world map. Returning home from his journey to Hindustan in the early fifth century, Faxian boarded a merchant vessel at that very port. Later, Yijing crossed the bay with ease, sailing smoothly from Sumatra to Tamralipti. So why should the Prince alone be unable to do the same?

At the mercy of the sea, things often fail to go according to plan. Needless to say, the Prince's ship never made it to Tamralipti. Instead, it wound up worlds away. Several days after leaving port, as the Andaman Islands reflected in the water to starboard, a powerful westerly wind blew their vessel back to land once more. The Prince and the others found themselves beached on the coast of an alien realm—one covered completely in jungle. Still, in a sense, the travelers could count themselves blessed. Their new ship, now stripped of its mast and rudder, was leaking and rapidly taking on water. They made land only moments before it sank.

"Yet another strange place! Why is it that things never go as planned? At this rate, we'll never reach Hindustan. We'll wander these seas forever. I simply can't believe it!"

These were the Prince's words, but he looked in no way dismayed. Perhaps he had already grown accustomed to such setbacks. Was he even—smiling?

"Now, where are we? The thick jungle suggests that this place sees a great deal of rain."

Engaku surveyed the area.

"From the looks of it, I'd say we're somewhere in the kingdom of Pyu. Then again, I hear that Pyu has recently fallen to Nanzhao in the north. The barbarians have since formed a new realm called Pagan, so perhaps Pyu is no longer the proper name for this place."

As the travelers headed cautiously into the jungle, their eyes were immediately filled with green. Endless stands of bamboo stretched skyward, leaving them breathless. But what kind of bamboo could this be? Some of the stalks probably measured thirty centimeters in diameter! They made the Sagano grove seem but a small and pale imitation. Struck by the spectacle, the Prince remarked:

"A stunning forest of bamboo if ever I've seen one. Even in the Southern Lands, I would never have believed bamboo could grow to such a size. Engaku, this must astonish even you."

Engaku blinked.

"Yes, Miko. That said, it's not entirely without precedent. In *The Chronicles of Huayang*, there is a Yunnanese variety of bamboo in which the distance between nodes can reach up to three meters. In fact, seeing this, I have to wonder if we're closer to Yunnan than we thought."

As Anten listened, he started digging up bamboo shoots with Akimaru's assistance. They hadn't realized it earlier, but there were numerous shoots pushing up through the jungle soil. The travelers had been at sea for days, and they were starving for fresh vegetables. They eyed the shoots eagerly, but could they eat them? Nothing about the whitish matter concealed within the hard sheaths seemed to suggest otherwise.

Just then, as they dug, a bell jangled behind them, and an odd-looking figure appeared. Completely naked, he had the body of a man and stood on two legs as people do, but his hairy head was that of a dog. He had pointy ears and long whiskers on his muzzle. Was he human or not? The four travelers were staring at this dog-headed man in utter astonishment when he opened his mouth to speak:

"What do you think you're doing, digging up those bamboo shoots?"

To their surprise, the dog-headed man's Tang speech was impeccable. Anten answered sharply:

"We want to eat them, obviously. Doesn't *Phyllostachys edulis* ring a bell?"

The strange man convulsed with laughter.

"One can hardly account for the taste of panda bears, to be sure, but for men to eat bamboo shoots willingly! Well, I never. . . . Hahaha!"

When the man laughed, they heard the same bell sound as before. Perhaps the bell was somewhere on his hirsute body. Although hidden from sight, its presence was betrayed with every chuckle.

The man's laughter showed no signs of abating. Soon Anten lost what little patience he had. He took a step toward the man and demanded:

"Stop your laughing! Tell me, what do you call this realm?"

Blankly, the man asked back:

"This realm?"

"Yes, what is the name of this realm? Surely it's no kingdom of dogs! Speak now, what is its name?"

The man looked rather serious now.

"If that's what you want to know, I'll tell you. This is the kingdom of Arakan, overlooking the Bay of Bengal. It stretches up the coast, with its back to a massive mountain range that runs north and south. Over the mountains are Pyu and Nanzhao, two realms locked in neverending combat, yet the effects of their fighting seldom reach this side of the mountains. For five centuries now, ever since Arakan was founded by the first of the Chandra kings, this remote territory has remained free from the yoke of its belligerent neighbors. In this way, our land has maintained its own history. Take our kings, for example, each of whom ends his name with Chandra. With a mountain wall behind us, we live largely in isolation; at the same time, the ocean opens in front of us, making Arakan a vital relay point in the sea lane linking east and west. Traders from Arabia and Persia often pass through our ports."

"Then you must have some special wares that appeal to these foreign merchants."

"Nothing of the sort. Arakan produces nothing of value, but if you go over the mountains and follow the Irrawaddy all the way upstream, you will find Yunnan. Nestled among its steep summits lies a mountain-locked utopia. For centuries, the route linking these lands has been traversed by traders with horses and oxen. In other words, before they can reach the rest of the world, Yunnanese treasures commonly pass through the ports along the Arakan coast."

"And what are these rare finds?"

"Well, to begin with, musk and kuth. Yunnan also produces jade, as well as amber, the sorts of commodities that will make any merchant salivate. Still, we Arakanese play no part in these lucrative transactions. All we can do is stand by and watch as foreign boats loaded with precious cargo sail off to distant lands."

Overcome by another sudden fit of laughter, the man began to shake. Sure enough, the bell started to ring again between his legs. No longer able to contain his curiosity, Anten pointed toward the source of the sound and asked:

"Beg your pardon, but why do you have a bell dangling from your private parts? Moments ago, you were laughing at us for eating bamboo shoots, but—in all seriousness—aren't you the odd one here?"

Mocked thus by Anten, the dog-headed man gazed sadly at his own body and replied:

"You mean this? I have to wear it—so dictates Arakanese law. I have no say in the matter. These damned bells shall haunt us until the day we die."

"And why is that?"

Looking as if he wanted to shrink away in shame, the man explained:

"The story is a long one indeed, but I will make it short. About a hundred years ago, during the reign of one Chandra king or another, a lascivious wind swept across this land. In that age, women regularly enjoyed the company of dogs. It was even considered a refined pastime for ladies of nobility. Consequently, quite a few men were born into this world with dogs' heads. There soon came a time in which maybe one in five Arakanese was born dog-headed. Distraught by the spreading dissipation, the Chandra King decided to slaughter every dog in the realm to keep things from getting any worse. Still, even if the dogs themselves were eliminated, as long as the dog-headed men survived, the possibility of miscegenation could hardly be ruled out. On the contrary, it was all too likely. So the King introduced a sort of chastity belt of his own devising, intended to nullify the reproductive capabilities of dog-headed men. That would be none other than this accursed bell. Men with dog heads are legally required to wear these until death. Thus we cannot know a woman's touch and, by extension, cannot sire children. The King thereby succeeded in putting a stop to things—by punishing the blameless dog-headed men. Clearly, we got the short end of the stick! Why, I ask you, should children pay the price for the depravity of their mothers?"

"Yes, quite right."

"It's an embarrassment. I wish I could hide it from the world, but word will inevitably get out. A day will come when tales of a Kingdom of Dog-Headed Men reach every corner of the world. It's already set in stone, I'm afraid."

"Come now, don't be so pessimistic. No one knows what the future will hold . . ."

Anten said this, but the dog-headed man merely stared into the distance, apparently inconsolable.

"Sadly, I know well what the future holds. Not to ring my own bell, so to speak, but we dog-headed men are endowed with a sense unique to our kind—I see the future as clearly as I see you now. I can see the world four hundred years from now. Famous explorers with strange names like Marco Polo, Odoric, Carpini, and Hayton will come from Europe. Ibn Battuta will come from Arabia. All of them will pass by Arakan on horse or by ship. Then, returning home, they will repeat snatches of rumor for the waiting ears of the world. On top of that, an audacious Englishman assuming the name of Mandeville will peddle similar tales without even setting foot outside Europe. Can you imagine? Of all things! To add insult to injury, a handful of these outsiders will refer to the realm of Arakan as the Andamans or the Nicobars. Then again, that's hardly surprising, considering the barefaced recklessness of these self-styled explorers."

At this point, Anten had heard enough of the man's long-winded harangue.

"Your visions of the future four centuries from now are little more than dreams to us, no more substantial than clouds."

Then Engaku jumped in:

"Another anachronism, staring us right in the face. This is like people in the Caribbean watching Columbus make landfall and saying, 'Hey, look! It's Columbus! We're discovered!' Enough of this. We're wasting our time. Let's keep moving."

Exasperated by the dog-headed man and his interminable jabbering, the four travelers excused themselves, offering him only a cursory farewell. As they walked away, his laughter followed them. Amid the pathetic mongrel howls, they could still hear that bell ringing between his legs.

AS ARAKAN HAD LONG been frequented by Brahmins and ruled by generations of Chandra kings, the travelers had hoped to find Buddhism in full flower there—yet this did not appear to be the case. Accordingly, there was little chance that the Arakanese King would provide the group with a new vessel as the Governor had so generously done in Panpan. After consulting with Anten and Engaku, the Prince decided that the best course of action would be to speak with the Arab traders and ask if they might ride west with them.

Now, the Arakan coast was quite long, but none of its seaports was truly worthy of the name. They were more like landings where ships happened to stop. Moreover, the merchants who sailed there tended to be a roguish and raffish bunch. Nonetheless, the travelers were set on reaching Hindustan, and beggars can't be choosers. One day, heading toward a nearby mooring, the Prince and the others came across the owner of a particular ship—one they'd had an eye on for some time. This man was a portly Arab by the name of Hassan. When the Prince mentioned to Hassan that he had come from Japan, Hassan displayed considerable interest:

"Well I'll be . . . al-Wāqwāq!"

The Prince had no idea what the man meant by these words.

"Sir, what is the meaning of this *whack-whack*?"

Hassan smiled.

"Oh, nothing. You know how the Tang call your land Woguo—meaning Dwarf Country, yes? Well, my people know it as al-Wāqwāq. That's all. Forget about that, though. You said you had a favor to ask?"

So the Prince told the man that he hoped to board his ship for Hindustan. Hassan stood there in silence for a few moments. Then a cunning grin formed on his lips and he said:

"Sure, friend, that's no problem at all. Still, there's this unwritten rule among seafarers like myself. I scratch your back, you scratch mine, get it? Now, looking at you, I'd have to guess you're a little light in the purse, am I right? Still, I think we can come to some sort of arrangement. You could give me a hand with my business, for example. You do that, and I'll be happy to give you a ride to Hindustan or any other 'stan of your choosing."

"And what is this business of yours?"

"Right, I'll tell you. I came here to hunt for honey men."

"Honey men? Never heard of them."

Hassan lowered his voice:

"Of course you haven't! Your average trader doesn't deal in such goods. To put it simply, honey men are bodies, human corpses, that have turned hard as rock. You probably know this already, but the Brahmins of old would sometimes renounce the world and head into the mountains. They'd stop eating and drinking there, too, living on nothing but honey. After a month or so, even their excrement would turn to honey. So, anyway, these Brahmins eventually died, but their bodies never decayed. On the contrary, they give off the most pleasant odor. In short, that's a honey man."

Listening to the Arab's explanation, the Prince suddenly remembered his old Master, who entered into nirvana in a cave on Mount Kōya. The Prince couldn't help but say his name aloud:

"Master Kūkai . . ."

"Did you say something?"

"Sorry, I was only thinking out loud. Please go on."

Hassan continued:

"I guess you're wondering what I want with these rock-hard corpses. Well, they offer the most miraculous medicinal properties. Grind up just a bit of a honey man and it'll cure any illness or injury in no time flat. I don't think I need to tell you this, but back in Baghdad, at the court of the Caliph, these bodies fetch prices that make the hunt well worth the trouble. And yes, hunting for honey men can be very troublesome. It takes a good amount of skill, and success is by no means guaranteed for those who go about it half-heartedly."

Now Anten cut in:

"You've mentioned 'hunting' a couple of times now, but where exactly do you 'hunt' for these bodies?"

"You know about the mountains that rise up behind the coast, right? Well, in the summer, the monsoon sweeps in from the Bay of Bengal and drenches everything this side of the mountains in the heaviest rain. The ground's almost always soaking wet here. But as soon as you crest the mountains, it isn't like that at all. The earth couldn't be drier. No trees, no grass, just fields and fields of honey men."

This time it was Engaku who spoke up skeptically:

"I was under the impression that the 'honey men' you spoke of were the sweet-smelling bodies of Brahmins who attained nirvana in mountain caves. If we're merely talking about the bodies scattered around some wasteland, what makes you think they're anything other than the corpses of common travelers?"

At this, the Arab made a face of sheer disgust.

"How the hell should I know? My job is to collect the honey men and transport them home. The pedigree of the deceased makes no difference to me. I'm not about to inspect the bodies! Brahmin or expired traveler, I could hardly care less."

Perhaps thinking it unwise to upset Hassan any further, the Prince artfully changed the subject:

"You said that hunting for honey men is not without some difficulty, yes? What did you mean by that?"

Hassan's face changed immediately.

"That's the thing. This wasteland is scorched by the sun, and the winds are always blowing fiercely. It isn't the sort of place that you can easily traverse on foot. If you're going to get safely in and out, you'll need to cover every inch of your body, to keep all the sand out of your face. Then you get into a canoe—a land canoe. It's on wheels and has a sail a good two meters high. Once you're in the canoe, you can get that wind working for you. At the same time, though, you pedal with your feet, as hard as you can. It takes a lot of work, believe me. Anyway, after a while, you'll reach the middle of the wasteland and see black bodies everywhere, all around you. So, how are you supposed to get them home? Well, this canoe is fitted with something like a claw. You catch the bodies on that and drag them out. Whatever you do, though, you can't get out of that canoe. If you set one foot outside, you're gone. The wasteland will start playing its tricks on you, and you'll never make it out alive."

"You mean, if something goes wrong, you wind up a honey man yourself?"

At the Prince's words, the Arab opened his eyes as wide as he could and nodded grandly.

"Well put, friend! Well put! Now you see why there are so many honey men out there. I should tell you, that's not the only danger involved in hunting for honey men. In fact, it gets much worse . . ."

"Much worse?"

Hassan paused a moment and peered into their faces, one by one. The Prince, Anten, Engaku, and then Akimaru. Taking his time, he began:

"You've heard of mirages, yes? They're well known at sea, but they can also occur in the hot swirling winds of the desert. Well, I don't know much about the meteorological conditions that cause these things, but they can happen out in the wasteland, too. You might not believe me, but, in the wasteland, every last honey man starts to look like a beautiful woman! Now, if it ended there, no problem, but you've been pedaling like mad, right? At some point, a strange feeling is going to hit you down there, if you know where I mean. Once that happens, the jig is up. Why, you ask? Like I was saying, you approach a body with the claw, and suddenly the honey man transforms into an irresistible woman! You do what you can to keep things under control but, in the end, you're going to ejaculate. Then the next body you see is another beautiful woman, and you ejaculate all over again. Now remember, there's no end to these seductive mirages. They're all around you. The more you pedal around, the more you ejaculate. Well, a man can only take so much of that before he's completely drained—hardly the ideal state for hunting."

The tale the Arab told was so incredible that the Prince and the others just stood there speechless, staring at him blankly. Then Hassan added casually:

"On this trip, I've already sent three young men out to hunt, but—just my luck—every one of them was helpless against these visions. No one's pulled a single honey man out yet. One of these boys, I don't know what happened to him, he went in and never came out. The other two managed to make it back physically unharmed, but I can hardly say the same for their minds. They're practically catatonic."

"What a shame . . ."

"Yeah, it's a shame, but that's how it is. They sailed with me to Arakan to hunt, but now I'm short-handed and have no bodies to show for it. I can't just go home empty-handed like this. . . . It's a damned disgrace."

At this point, Hassan stopped and looked into their faces again, one by one. It was almost as if he was waiting for them to solve some sort of riddle. After a moment, Anten spoke up:

"So, you want the four of us to go out there and bring you back some honey men? These are your terms?"

"Well, in a nutshell . . ."

Anten answered unequivocally:

"We won't do it. No seeker of the Dharma would ever sink so low! It's absurd . . ."

But the Prince restrained him quietly:

"Hold on, Anten. Let's not be so hasty. We ought to discuss the matter in private, just among ourselves."

They told the man that they needed a moment to talk things

over, and walked away. The grinning Arab watched them from
the deck of his ship.

Once the travelers were alone, Anten immediately gave the
Prince a piece of his mind:

"Miko, this is no laughing matter. Don't tell me you're
seriously considering doing mercenary work for this skinflint
trader! I understand that we need help to make our way to Hindustan, I do, but surely you understand how wrong it would be
for a monk to involve himself in such unseemly labor!"

Engaku added:

"Anten's right. This scoundrel led us to believe that these
so-called honey men were Brahmins, but as it turns out, they're
merely the blackened bodies of common travelers! Needless to
say, the 'medicinal properties' he mentioned are dubious at best.
Miko, please think this through."

Akimaru had said nothing until then, but now joined in:

"Miko, nothing good can come from such dealings. It won't
get us any closer to Hindustan. In fact, it could cost us everything we have."

When the three of them were done speaking, the Prince
responded:

"There's no need to get so worked up. When the Arab first
mentioned the honey men, I was quite unexpectedly reminded
of my mentor, Master Kūkai. That's all. Of course, on Mount
Kōya, he didn't have any honey. He simply set aside all sustenance and focused fully on meditation. Still, I suppose Master
Kūkai was a honey man of a kind."

"But Miko, these honey men are of no such noble
background."

"What difference does that make? In death, all shall realize their Buddha nature. Nonetheless, I would like to see this
wasteland and its honey men, in order to reflect on impurity."

"Impurity?"

"Yes, I've had some training in such matters. That being the case, I doubt there's any chance I could ever mistake a honey man for a beautiful woman! I feel I can say that much with confidence. In fact, seeing those blackened corpses with one's own eyes is quite an opportunity for a seeker of the Dharma. Believe me, there's no need to worry. I'll cross the mountains on my own; the rest of you shall stay here in safety. I, for one, wish to know more about these honey men."

Once the Prince had spoken, there was little the others could do but entertain his whims.

Apparently, Hassan had expected either Anten or Engaku to venture into the wasteland. When he learned that the Prince, the eldest member of the group, would go alone, he held his tongue—but his face still revealed his astonishment.

What Hassan had called the land canoe was about three meters long and sat on a pair of wooden wheels. It had to be pedaled, not unlike a bicycle. The ground was rock hard, so there was no danger of the wheels getting jammed in loose earth. When the two-meter sail caught enough wind, the canoe would apparently glide across the ground like a speedboat. Who knows who had invented this clever contraption, but it certainly was the best way to travel through the area.

Beyond the mountains, the land rose and fell like a choppy sea. As Hassan had said, there was not a single plant in sight, only a scorched ocean of sand shaped by tremendously powerful winds. The air was stifling, and objects appeared to double or triple in the heat. Clearly, the trader was not wrong: Entering this barren land required no small amount of resolve.

Covered from head to toe in a protective suit of woven bamboo strips, the Prince took his seat inside the canoe in the highest of spirits. It was noon at the time. Thanks to the wind, the slightest pressure on the pedals sent the canoe racing. Indeed, it moved so easily that the Prince was almost taken aback. The wind howled in his ears as it sped forward, rocking from side to side. The Prince was intoxicated by the speed as he surrendered to the motion of the canoe. Then it hit him: Doesn't this feel a little too good? If I keep going like this, who knows where the pleasure will take me? He told himself he had to be careful, but, strangely, the more he thought about it, the more pleasurable it felt.

Worried by this, the Prince rubbed the rosary beads he always carried with him, faced south, and prayed. *Praise be to Mahavairocana, praise be to Mahavairocana, praise be to Mahavairocana.* Immediately, the Prince's fears vanished, and the canoe, which had been racing along the ground, suddenly lifted into the air. With the wind in its sail, the vehicle rose and fell gently, as if at sea. From his new vantage point, the Prince could see countless specks below. Honey men, no doubt. He strained his eyes to get a better look at the tiny black figures.

The trader had warned the Prince that the honey men would appear to be beautiful, but nothing could have been further from the truth. The remains scattered throughout the wasteland were unquestionably human—and grotesque beyond description. Some had human heads but animal bodies, some had bodies but no heads, some had only half a body, some had two heads, some had three, some had heads with no faces, some had faces with no heads, some had three eyes, some had no hands, some had too many legs, some were no more than skeletons, some were covered entirely in fur, some had holes in their bellies, some had tails, some had heads with lips that drooped down to the hard black earth, some had ears bigger than their heads, some had eyes that had popped completely out of their sockets. All were cadaveric odds and ends of this variety.

As the Prince looked down over the wasteland from the flying canoe, he felt that he had confronted impurity on the highest level. He was glad he had come to see the honey men. He now felt that much closer to nirvana. The Prince was so satisfied that he actually wanted to thank the trader for presenting him with the unusual opportunity. Feeling refreshed, he pedaled on, leaving the wasteland behind.

By this time, the canoe had gone well beyond Arakan's borders. The Prince was sailing over the Irrawaddy and following it farther and farther upstream. How many hours had it been since he had stepped into the canoe? Looking ahead, beyond a blanket of white, he saw the majestic mountains that bear the name Yunnan: "South of the Clouds." The Prince couldn't say why, but the sight filled him with a kind of nostalgia, as if he were heading home. His heart raced at the thought. Could this rickety flying canoe make it over the clouds to Yunnan? Only one way to find out. The Prince kept pedaling as the canoe flew due northeast, straight toward Yunnan, sailing right over the mountaintops.

He crossed the Irrawaddy, the Salween, and the Mekong. Between the layers of mountains, he spotted a lake in the distance that shone like a mirror. It had to be Lake Er, at the center of the Dali Basin. Beside the lake were the green Cang Mountains, beyond which the Prince could make out the stony spires of Mount Cock-Claw. At last, thought the Prince, I've arrived in Yunnan. Although the Prince had left at noon, the sun was now starting to set, its scarlet rays turning the surrounding mountains purple. The Prince took in the whole scene from far above.

In moments like this, the Prince tended to get sleepy. Perhaps the canoe ride had left him feeling unexpectedly relieved. Luckily, the sail was now full of wind and the vessel was flying steadily, so the Prince figured he could stop pedaling without fear of falling to the earth below. He decided to curl up inside the peapod-shaped canoe and close his eyes—just for a little while.

The moment he did, he began to dream. It no longer bears repeating, but dreaming was something at which the Prince was particularly adept.

IN HIS DREAM, THE Prince was in his mid-thirties. For some reason, he had climbed to the top of a tall cedar. Why had he done such a thing? He couldn't be sure. Soon the sun set, and he was overcome by a peculiar kind of loneliness, so he made his way down the trunk. At the base of the tree, he found himself surrounded by buildings, all kinds of pagodas and halls in the midst of construction. This was Mount Kōya, he thought. Mount Kōya not long after Kūkai had started living there, a place the Prince knew well. I should say hello, the Prince thought, making his way to the only illuminated hall in sight.

Peering inside, the Prince saw Kūkai, apparently in the middle of some kind of ritual. Lanterns were glowing red, a sacred fire was burning; on the altar, he had placed a variety of objects, including peacock feathers, a cross-shaped vajra, and a statue of a peacock with the Wisdom King Mahāmāyūrī on its back.

Kūkai was sitting in front of these objects in deep contemplation, chanting dhāraṇīs. At that moment, he spun around and greeted the Prince:

"Well, well! If it isn't the Zen Prince. How good of you to visit."

But when Kūkai turned around, the Prince could see that this was not the face of a living man. He looked more like a gilded wooden statue, with rock-crystal eyes, hard and expressionless.

Alas, the Prince thought, the Master has known his time of death and denied himself all forms of grain; he must be drinking some sort of cinnabar elixir. This transformed face was too much for the Prince to bear, so he turned away. Yet Kūkai did not seem particularly disturbed by the Prince's reaction. He simply asked, mockingly:

"You've been climbing trees again, haven't you? Well, did you see anything from the top?"

As Kūkai laughed, the Prince found himself laughing along.

"You see everything, Master. No, I didn't. I suppose I've always been fond of high places."

"Yes, places both high and far. No doubt you thought you might be able to see distant Hindustan from that high up?"

The Prince had never thought of it that way, but Kūkai was probably right.

"That might be it . . ."

"I'm sure I've never met anyone else like you. From what I've observed, your mind is always somewhere else—some faraway land. When I was only a boy, I traveled to Khitai, but couldn't continue as far as Hindustan. You, on the other hand, are intent on going through with this, aren't you?"

"Who knows what the future will hold . . ."

"No, there's no mistaking it. From what I can see, you will head toward Hindustan—but you will never arrive. For a time, you will travel through the Southern Lands, where fortune will smile on you. In fact, I wish I could accompany you on your future voyage, but illness has wasted me, and my days are numbered."

"Master . . ."

"You know, I've given a lot of thought to the idea of putting you in charge of Mount Kōya, but I've decided against it. After all, your ambitions are clearly too great to be contained within the narrow confines of Japan! I'd be happy to leave this place to you, but you would soon wander off to Hindustan or some such land, which would only make things more difficult for whoever would take your place. Isn't that true, Lord Monk?"

Kūkai appeared to be smiling, but his face was only shining like a metal mask—there was no human emotion to be found there.

Just then, behind Kūkai, the Prince thought he saw the peacock statue on the altar twitch its long, speckled neck and fan out its colorful plumage. He could not help doubting his eyes. Yet when he got a better look at the proud bird, the Prince was surprised to find that it had the face of a human woman—Kusuko's face, to be precise. Kusuko must have had some deep connection with winged animals, as she had so often assumed the form of a bird in the Prince's dreams. Now, in death, she seemed to have stolen into the holy grounds of Mount Kōya, where women were strictly forbidden, disguising herself as the mount of the Peacock King. Was Kūkai aware of this?

Meanwhile, the peacock seemed to sense the Prince's gaze. It tilted its head to one side and let out a barely audible cry: *kha kha kha kha kha!*

Kūkai also heard the bird and turned around to beckon the creature.

Slowly, the peacock lowered its clawed feet from the altar. As it did, the figure of the Wisdom King on the bird's back suddenly disappeared from view. No, it hadn't vanished—the Prince had taken its place. He was riding the giant bird now. Who could say when it had happened, but the Prince and the Wisdom King had become indistinguishable.

These things happen often enough in the realm of dreams.

"Goodbye, Lord Monk. Though it may not be in Hindustan, you and I shall cross paths again. Believe me."

At these words from Kūkai, the peacock flapped its wings and rose gently into the sky over Mount Kōya with the Prince on its back.

From that height, the Prince thought he saw the five-ringed stupas that stood at the edge of the black cedar forest surrounding the Oku-no-in. But how could that be? Wasn't Kūkai alive just now? How strange! Clearly, time in the Prince's dream was unhinged. Come to think of it, it was some thirty years ago—forty-nine days after the Master's death—that the Prince carried his master's body down the very path over which he now flew. Remembering that day, he looked below.

There, the Prince saw six monks carrying a coffin, followed by an antlike procession, moving silently and solemnly. The six men were Kūkai's closest disciples. The Prince knew them all: There's Jitsue, and Shinzen, and Shinshō, and Shinga, and Shisai—and the last of them was none other than the Prince himself. Seeing this, he let out a sharp cry. There was some distance between them, but the Prince had never seen his own face in a dream.

As if in response to his cry, the peacock raised its voice again: *kha kha kha kha kha!*

With that harsh sound, the Prince was brought back to the waking world. He was certain he'd been on the back of a large peacock, but he now found himself back inside the flying canoe.

LAKE ER, SO CALLED because it takes the shape of a human ear, was once known as Lake Kunming, and can be found in the very center of the Dali Basin, to the immediate east of the Cang Mountains. The area was inhabited by a barbarian tribe formerly known as the Er—or, alternatively, the Kunming. In either case, their name was a nod to that beautiful body of water. From the time of the late Han dynasty, the Kunming were given the name Ailao; later, during the Tang dynasty, they were called the Baiyi. When the nation of Nanzhao was founded in the eighth century, it was made up mostly of the farming Baiyi, and to a lesser extent the nomadic Wuman of the mountains. Then again, as the Meng Clan who ruled Nanzhao were Wuman, it may be more accurate to say that it was the Wuman who stood at the center of the nation.

The Lolo are often made to represent the whole of the Wuman, but it is worth noting that the name Wuman refers to multiple groups of people—a wide variety of minorities whose languages belong to the Tibeto-Burman family, including the Moso and the Lisu.

Mention has already been made of the Chandra name in Arakan tradition. Curiously, however, the practice of the Nanzhao royals was to link their names together like a daisy chain, the tail of one king's name becoming the head of the next. This Wuman custom can be seen in the names of the first eight generations of Nanzhao kings: Xinuluo, Luosheng, Shengluopi, Piluoge, Geluofeng, Fengjiayi, Yimouxun, Xungequan, Quanlongsheng. Notably, Fengjiayi died before assuming the throne, making Yimouxun the sixth king of Nanzhao.

Approaching the auriform lake, the Prince directed his flying canoe just over the Cang Mountains and landed near the top of Mount Cock-Claw. This mountain owes its name to the curious arrangement of its peaks: three points up front and one in the back, resembling the claw of a bird.

Night had broken and given way to a new morning. The Prince had no clear goal when he landed on the mountain, but

the dream from which he'd only recently awoken had yet to settle within him. Maybe, he thought, I can meet Master Kūkai
here. It was an inexplicable instinct, a hunch with no reason-
ing behind it whatsoever—and perhaps that was exactly why it
deserved his faith.

The craggy peaks of Mount Cock-Claw had been eroded
by powerful winds and rainstorms, making them much steeper
than anything found in Japan. Morning mist circled the rocks,
drifting between the cliff walls. The Prince let the mountain
air fill his chest. As he walked on, he saw drawings of what
appeared to be female genitalia, suggesting that this path had
been traveled by people throughout the ages. As with the lingam
in Chenla, these graphic depictions failed to shock the Prince in
any way.

In his own day, the Ming-dynasty traveler Xu Xiake wrote,
"Mount Cock-Claw offers a view of the world in its entirety,"
and the Prince's view from the top was truly kaleidoscopic—
yet that scenery meant nothing to him now. He was too busy
searching, looking for something. And what was that? What did
he want? The Prince couldn't be sure. Looking back on it now,
he felt that his entire life had been one endless search. Where
would it end? What could possibly provide him with final satisfaction? When the Prince considered this, he felt that he already
knew exactly what it was he'd been seeking. He had the sense
that nothing would surprise him now, not one bit. Whatever he
found at the end of his journey would only inspire him to say:
"Of course—just as I'd imagined."

Walking along the edge of the dizzying precipice, the Prince
made his way through a series of stone archways; then, heading
behind the summit, he discovered a cave carved into the rock
that looked as if it must have been there for centuries. A gate

of rotting wood stood at the mouth. Without a moment's hesitation, the Prince forced his way inside. Immediately, a thick mist filled his eyes, leaving him unable to see so much as an inch ahead.

Stupefied, the Prince waited for the mist to dissipate. When it did, he saw something: a niche hewn out of the rock, within which he saw what appeared to be a man sitting in the lotus position, his hands forming the Vairocana mudra. The body was coated with lacquer and had been fitted with crystal eyes. Although the face was no longer that of a living man, it looked startlingly similar to that of Kūkai—the Kūkai from the dream he had just seen. Somehow, it seemed, the two of them had been reunited.

The Prince had awoken from that dream only moments ago, but he couldn't help feeling that it was worlds away from him now—as if it were a dream from the distant, distant past.

"At last, we meet again, Master. It would seem you were right as always. There could be no greater joy than this . . ."

The Prince said these words and bowed deeply before the honey man, wiping away his tears with his sleeve.

# MIRROR LAKE

The mountain-bound nation of Nanzhao was different in every sense from the realms along the South Sea through which the Prince had already passed. First, there was the climate. As the Ming poet Yang Shen wrote of this region after he was exiled to Yunnan for displeasing Emperor Jiajing: "Flowering branches unending, in every season spring." Here it was neither hot nor cold but always mild. This alone made it a much more hospitable place. Additionally, while Yunnan had long taken advantage of the Burma Route to trade with India, the area was much more exposed to cultural influences from China. Local government and religious practices, for example, were entirely based on Chinese models. The same could be said of its Buddhist temples. In this sense, the area differed markedly from Chenla, Funan, and Panpan, all of which were under the strong influence of Indian culture. From the age of Piluoge, Nanzhao's fourth ruler, who was dubbed King of Yunnan by Emperor Xuanzong, the Nanzhao royals felt no need to disguise their outright Sinophilia. Time and again, China-crazed Nanzhao marched on Chengdu, robbing the Han of their riches and their craftsmen. The nation also repeatedly pressed the Tang court to wed their princesses into the Nanzhao royal bloodline, and for the nation's young aristocrats, there was no dream as fine as studying in Chengdu.

In *The New Book of Tang*, we learn that it was Fengyou, the tenth ruler of Nanzhao, who put an end to the custom of kingly names, stating: "It is out of my love for China that I cannot in good faith continue my father's name." Thus, in his reign, this tradition was abandoned. Perhaps King Fengyou felt that nothing could be more embarrassing than participating in some childish name game.

At any rate, the Prince had paid his respects to the honey

man resting in the cave atop Mount Cock-Claw. His heart now at peace, he began his descent. In his travels so far, the Prince had always been in the company of Anten, Engaku, and young Akimaru. Finding himself alone in a foreign land for the first time, he looked inward, wondering if he felt at all lonely. He was certain he did not. In fact, as he made his way downhill and saw the spring flowers covering the green mountainside, the Prince felt lighter, as if he were a young man again. This sort of setting was far from common in the sun-scorched Southern Lands, and as the Prince went on, a peculiar fantasy took hold of him: Had he returned to his native Japan?

An odd thought now bubbled within him. He felt as though he had left his real self behind—or that some part of him had come loose. But how? Was it this place or was it something inside him? Whichever the case, it was as if his original self had been left back in Arakan with his fellow travelers; meanwhile, another Prince had traveled up to Nanzhao by flying canoe. It was an unsettling feeling, but he felt as light as a feather, as if he had been released from the fetters of the self and was now wandering free. He did his best to think positively, telling himself he should try to enjoy this newfound sense of freedom.

Arriving at the foothills, the Prince came upon a cave hidden behind some rocks. On the ground by the cave was something that caught his eye. At first, he thought it might be the dead body of a brightly colored bird. Drawing closer, however, the Prince could see it was not a bird but a pair of wings large enough to fit a human. In the sun, they looked dark blue. The beautiful feathers brought to mind the harem in Chenla where the Prince had encountered the half-bird women, each with feathers of a different color. Nevertheless, what he saw here was neither bird nor woman—only wings, with no body in sight.

The Prince approached the wings to pick them up, but discovered upon touching them that they were soaking wet.

Sensing a presence behind him, the Prince turned toward the entrance of the cave. Whoever had been there must have noticed him and retreated to cover. Out of the corner of his eye, the Prince thought he had seen a half-naked child. Most likely a girl, judging from the style of her hair—maybe thirteen or so? The sun was burning brightly and everything was perfectly still, almost like in a daydream.

Curiosity rose within the Prince, so he hid behind a large tree and waited for the girl to reemerge. He was certain she would. After all, she had probably come to collect the wings. Sure enough, a moment later, she stuck her head out of the cave and made a mad dash toward the wings, grabbed them, then ran back to the cave as quickly as she could.

Seeing this, the Prince arrived at the following thought: The wings were wet, so the girl had placed them outside to dry in the sun, but soon worrying about leaving them unattended, she ran back outside to claim them. When she came out a second time to find her wings untouched, she must have been relieved. The spectacular wings were evidently a prized possession of hers.

Approaching the black cave, the Prince peered inside. He debated for a moment whether to follow the girl, but finally he stepped into its shadowy mouth.

Before he could take ten paces, all sunlight had vanished. It was so dark that even if someone were about to pinch his nose, he wouldn't have seen it coming. Inching forward with one hand on the cave wall, the Prince followed the path as it twisted to the left and to the right until he eventually lost all sense of direction. By this point, he had gone so far into the cave that he could no longer hear any sounds from the outside world. Then the Prince noticed the smallest dot of light within the otherwise perfect dark. In the wall was an opening—just large enough for a child to squeeze through. The light was coming from the other side.

The Prince put his eye up to the opening and looked through. A flame was burning inside, brightening a large space. Against the far wall of that hidden cavern sat the girl, now wearing the wings. The Prince had the impression that she was trying to dry them using both the heat of the fire and her own body. She occasionally gave the wings a flap, and when she did her shadow on the wall looked like a giant bat in flight.

The Prince stood by the hole and studied the girl for some time. The flame grew stronger, and he finally got a good view of her face. In disbelief, he mouthed the words:

"Is that you, Akimaru? But how . . . ?"

The Prince was convinced she was indeed Akimaru. The longer he looked at the girl, the greater the resemblance became. The Prince asked himself repeatedly: How could this child not be Akimaru? Deciding he was probably in the middle of a dream, he did his best to slip through the small opening in the cave wall, but quickly discovered it was impossible. Maybe if his shoulders and hips were as skinny as the girl's—but his frame being what it was, the Prince could go no farther.

That being the case, he thrust his head through the hole, which gave the child quite a scare. She stepped back against the far wall and shrieked in some incomprehensible tongue. This alone should have told the Prince that the girl could not have been Akimaru, but he found it difficult to shake his initial impression. Without knowing whether the Tang language would hold any meaning for the frightened girl, the Prince spoke to her through the hole:

"Don't be afraid. I would never do anything to hurt you.

Even if I wanted to, how could I fit through this little hole? That aside, I cannot help feeling as though I know you well. You remind me of a child who has traveled with me from Guangzhou. So let me ask—is there any chance you have a long-lost sister?"

The girl was visibly confused, seemingly unable to understand what the Prince was saying. In fact, she appeared more terrified now that this strange man was trying to talk to her.

The two of them looked at each other from across the hole in the weak light of the flames. How long did that go on? The girl now appeared to have calmed somewhat. Although she was no longer paralyzed with fear, she didn't seem to be entirely comfortable with the Prince's presence. Watching her, he began to feel her anxiousness rubbing off on him.

Perhaps worn out at last from the strain of her constant vigil, the girl began to nod off, giving the Prince a better chance to observe her face in full. Once she was asleep, her anxious features relaxed into something resembling a smile. As he stared at the sleeping girl, the Prince's confused mind was filled with a series of thoughts that formed and drifted away like clouds.

Yes—Engaku had told the Prince in private that Akimaru likely had Lolo blood. Those same features were just as clear in this child. For one thing, she had the same almond-shaped eyes supposedly common among the Lolo. And they lay perfectly level, slanting neither upward nor downward, just like Akimaru's. Since Nanzhao had a large Lolo population, it wasn't so strange to find a girl who resembled Akimaru here, but the similarity between them was all too striking. Perhaps, as the Prince had imagined earlier, the two were twins? What if circumstances had led to them becoming separated at a young age? What if Akimaru had been sold into slavery and trafficked through distant lands, while her sister had been brought up all those years as a Yunnanese girl? Indeed, what other explanation could there be? While the Prince understood how incredible it sounded, looking at the girl now, he couldn't imagine it being otherwise.

How could I look at the child and not think she was Akimaru? Since I named her Akimaru, "Autumn Child," I'll call this one Harumaru—"Spring Child." What a joyous thing it would be to bring this girl to where Akimaru waits, to reunite them! And think how astonished Anten and Engaku would look! Seeing each other for the first time, how would Akimaru and Harumaru react? The Prince's thoughts continued to unfold in this way, until he eventually realized the girl's fire had gone out. The cave was completely and utterly dark.

Just then, the Prince heard heavy footfalls coming his way. Several men burst in with torches, shouting in a barbarian tongue. One of the torches lit up the Prince's face and he winced, his eyes having grown accustomed to the dark.

Were these men Nanzhao officials? They examined the Prince with an air of self-importance and shoved their torches through the hole by which he stood, easily locating the girl curled up against the wall of the chamber within. The girl must have wakened at the sound of the men marching in. Now stiff with fear, she backed her winged body against the far wall.

Finding the girl there, the men cried for joy, which the Prince took to mean that they had traveled all the way to Mount Cock-Claw to retrieve her. *Let us rejoice, we've finally found our girl*—the Prince thought he could detect such a message in their indecipherable cries.

They waved their torches menacingly until the girl admitted defeat and squeezed back through the hole, but as she did, she immediately latched onto the Prince, which surprised no one more than the Prince himself. Maybe the girl knew that she could rely on him and him alone. Or perhaps something akin to familiarity had grown within her during the hours they had spent staring at one another in the dark. At any rate, the Prince found himself quite moved by this. He wrapped his arms around her shoulders, wings and all, assuring her:

"I don't know what's going on here, Harumaru, but don't lose faith. I'll get you out of this mess."

Overhearing the Prince's Tang, an older man in a tight-fitting leather cuirass—apparently the group's commanding officer—addressed the Prince in the same language:

"Judging from your appearance, I had you pegged as a foreigner. So, tell me, what is your relation to this young girl?"

The Prince stood tall.

"I've only just met her. I have no idea what sort of crime the child has committed. I am a monk from Japan, traveling to Hindustan in search of the Dharma. I have come through Chang'an, where I received the imperial stamp of the Great Tang Emperor."

"You say you've come from Chang'an?"

"Not directly. I stayed in the Tang empire for over two years and spent half a year of that in Chang'an."

Hearing the Prince say this, the man quickly changed his attitude. He now paid the Prince no small amount of respect. His language became polite, practically sycophantic:

"I beg your pardon, sir. I was unaware. My name is Meng Jianying. I am a distant relative of the King. In my youth, I was granted the opportunity to study in Chengdu, where I was fortunate enough to acquire some knowledge of the Tang language, yet embarrassingly I have not yet had the chance to visit the capital. Now, as for this girl . . ."

Taking a step toward the Prince and gesturing toward the frightened child, the man named Meng went on:

"She was chosen from among the people to dance exclusively for the court. As a dancing girl, she'd put on her wings and perform at palace banquets and so on. But she recently ran away, leaving not so much as a feather behind. Fortunately, we have caught up with her here, so we can now take her back to the castle, where some severe punishment surely awaits. I strongly doubt she'll be keeping her ears . . ."

"Her ears?" the Prince cried.

At this, a grin appeared at the corners of Meng's mouth.

"Well, cutting off the ears is perhaps the simplest form of punishment in this realm. But talking here will get us nowhere. Let us leave this place. I am under royal orders to escort our young runaway back to the castle on the lake immediately. If it would please you, however, you are more than welcome to join us. We have transport at the ready, which will surely be much faster than walking."

The Prince had no desire to go to a strange castle with these men, but he was even less inclined to let them run off with the winged girl, so he agreed.

When the group emerged from the darkness of the cave, the sun was blinding. A number of horses—who knows where they'd gotten them—were grazing on the grass. At Meng's gesture, the Prince mounted one of the horses without hesitation. The girl, still wearing her glorious wings, did the same. She certainly didn't look like a criminal being charged with dereliction of duty—more like a costumed child playing a part in a parade. The girl appeared to be a skilled equestrian, perhaps having ridden horses from childhood. She easily outshone our Prince.

Traveling up and down a series of mountain passes, the

men cut farther and farther west across the foothills of Mount Cock-Claw until at last that mirror-like lake could be seen gleaming in the distance: Lake Er. It could hardly have looked less like the Tonle Sap. The lapping waves of silver and gold left the Prince breathless. How like that lake back in Ōmi, the Prince thought. Even the snow-capped peaks surrounding Lake Er evoked the mountains of Hiei, Hira, and Ibuki. So far from home, the Prince hardly expected to be reminded of some of his fondest memories—memories of a lake he had known so well since boyhood, memories forever connected to Kusuko. These thoughts in mind, the Prince now rode on, feeling overjoyed.

Meng pulled up to the Prince's side and said:

"This scene is known as Silver Peaks and Jeweled Waters; word of its beauty reaches even the Tang empire. By the way, there's something else for which this lake is famed. They say if you look into the water and see no reflection, you will die within the year. Of course, this is only a silly superstition, but that's what they say. I wouldn't believe it myself—not for a second."

At a trot, the riders traversed the path that sloped downward to the lake. When they reached the shore, the men dismounted and boarded rafts that had been waiting for them. These rafts were kept afloat with inflated leather bags but couldn't accommodate more than four men apiece, so they split into two groups.

As the vessels glided slowly toward the center of the lake, the Prince's nostalgic visions of Lake Biwa were projected over the scene. But this was no time for the Prince to lose himself in fond reminiscences. In the raft, which was so narrow that the passengers' knees nearly touched, Meng wouldn't stop speaking to him. Since Meng knew that the girl understood no Tang, he had no compunction about discussing her current predicament right in front of her:

"As I was saying before, the girl was chosen for the purpose of performing in the palace, but allow me to be more specific. Dancing girls are not exactly chosen at random from among the people of the nation. Our dancers are held to the strictest requirements. I suppose I need not mention that beauty is a must—at the same time, being beautiful alone is not sufficient. From antiquity, we've had a performance in this land called the bird dance, and a dancer must meet certain conditions to perform it. In early summer, when storms fill the sky, the nomad women of the Yunnan Mountains are touched by lightning and lay eggs. The palace dancers are one and all chosen from these egg-born girls. No, they're not exactly 'chosen.' The number of girls born in this way is decidedly small, so whenever word of a new egg reaches the ears of our officials, they quickly send an official from the court to ask the parents to raise this rare child in a manner befitting a court dancer. Needless to say, the girls must eventually live at the academy, where they are educated in all matters of courtly song and dance. And even if the parents should voice some objection to this, the officials are not likely to back down."

At the mention of eggs, an image bubbled up from the depths of the Prince's memory—that mysterious orb that Kusuko had thrown across the dark courtyard as she said the words "Away, away you go! Off to distant Hindustan." Yes, Kusuko was tired of being human. Didn't she say she wanted to be reborn as a bird in Hindustan? But who could have known that here in Yunnan, not Hindustan, women could be hatched from eggs? If what this man said was true, then perhaps Akimaru and Harumaru were born from the same egg! Now the Prince was even more confused than before, wild thoughts firing rapidly in his mind.

According to the sixth volume of Tan Cui's *Record of the Wilds of Yunnan*, there is a bird in Yunnan with the face of a woman—a bird known as the kalaviṅkā. Apparently, its call could be heard, but the bird itself was never seen. Now, if the Prince had read this, he would surely have concluded that Akimaru and Harumaru were two such creatures; unfortunately, however, the Prince had never read this book.

Whether or not Harumaru was aware that she was the topic of conversation, her face displayed only innocence as she sat there, absorbed in preening her wings. She looked every inch a bird. It was then the Prince realized that her wings had likely become wet from swimming across this very lake during her escape.

Meng continued:

"Some years, the lightning almost never stops; in other years, there may be a single bolt or two. There is also some degree of chance involved in a woman's conception, so in certain years the academy is brimming with candidates, and in others they've had to make do with only one or two. It's no different from harvesting crops, I suppose—there are years of plenty and years of scarcity. Such is the working of nature."

Yet something in Meng's story didn't add up. The Prince racked his brains, then muttered:

"Never in my life have I heard of conception by lightning."

Meng responded excitedly:

"Well, of course you have! It is the sound of thunder by which peacocks conceive. This is clearly stated in Buddhist scripture. Here in Nanzhao, even the reigning King Shilong was conceived when his mother was touched by lightning. This is widely known. Some say that his mother was bathing in Lake Er when she was touched by a dragon, but lightning is certainly capable of disguising itself as a dragon in order to get closer to a woman. More to the point, dragon or lightning, they serve the same purpose when it comes to the creation of life . . ."

Meng appeared animated as he spoke about such matters, but the Prince was unable to rid himself of the thought of Akimaru and Harumaru. Casually, he asked:

"When a woman is touched by lightning, does a single egg ever produce twins?"

"Twins? Well, I've never heard of such a thing. Though, I will say, twin dancers performing the bird dance would truly be something to see . . ."

On the subject of twins, Meng's tone was indifferent.

At last, the far shore of Lake Er came into view, with a magnificent castle that seemed to stretch from the foothills of the Cang Mountains to the edge of the lake. It was Dali Castle.

As the rafts approached, the Prince saw the blue tiles of the watchtower; he saw the castle gate and the long banners streaming down from it; he saw the covered path leading from the shore to the gate. He felt as if he could almost reach out and grab the spear-wielding guardsmen. The sunlight on the roof tiles set the whole city aglow in a beautiful blue light. There were buildings on the shore as well, outside the castle walls. Among the soaring structures were temples and pagodas, and in this way the Prince learned that Buddhism had flowered here in Nanzhao as well. His heart now at ease, the Prince remarked to Meng:

"What a splendid sight. King Shilong resides in the castle, I take it?"

"This castle has been home to the kings of Nanzhao since the days of Yimouxun, our sixth king. King Shilong resides here now—more so than any royal before him, in a manner of speaking. He is, you might say, a little eccentric. He's only just turned twenty, yet he and his mother, who is blessed with excellent health, almost never leave the castle."

"Hm. What do you mean by eccentric?"

"I'd best not say. You'll soon see with your own eyes, I

suppose, once we arrive at the castle. And I only mean to help, so please pay no mind if you find this advice objectionable, but if your heart is set on protesting on behalf of the dancer, then I suggest you take your case directly to the King. That would certainly be the most promising way to realize your goal. The King has long been infatuated with all things Chinese, and anyone who can speak in Tang and tell tales of Chang'an would have his way with ease. I daresay you will find your command of the Tang language to be your greatest weapon in all matters within our borders. Ah, here we are."

Before disembarking, the Prince happened to glance over the boat's side into the mirror-like lake without giving it any real thought. When he did, he saw no face in the water returning his gaze. He could see the reflection of those around him, clear as day—his reflection alone was missing. He looked several more times, but what he found was the same each time. According to what Meng had said earlier, anyone who did not see their own reflection in the water was bound to die within a year. The Prince had dismissed this as mere myth, but he still couldn't help feeling startled.

The others were busy preparing to go ashore, so they failed to notice. The Prince decided to bury this within his heart, telling not a soul.

Once on land, the dancing girl was dragged off in one direction by the officials, while the Prince was guided in another. She was surely headed for the dungeon. When they parted, the girl gave him a terribly sad look—an image that the Prince could not shake.

There were special quarters for foreign visitors within the castle, and this was where the Prince was taken. He was still worried about the girl's well-being but was so exhausted that he fell into a deep sleep moments after arriving.

That night, the Prince dreamed of Akimaru and Harumaru hand in hand, performing the bird dance. While the Eight Immortals of Kunlun was intended for a circle of four dancers, this bird dance was meant for only two, and it proceeded at a dizzying pace. As the Prince watched, the two spun around so swiftly that the Prince lost track of which girl was which. Unable to stand the confusion, the Prince demanded:

"Which one of you is Akimaru? Tell me now!"

The two responded in perfect unison:

"Me!"

"Well, which one of you is Harumaru? Tell me!"

Again, they answered:

"Me!"

Finally, the Prince gave up, at which point the dancers stopped spinning, looked at each other like a pair of birds, and broke into laughter.

THE NEXT MORNING, THE Prince awoke to the sound of someone knocking. When he stumbled out of bed and answered the door, Meng told him:

"It's time for the morning ceremony. This is surely a good opportunity for you to see the King."

Meng led the sleepy-eyed Prince down the long corridors of the castle until they finally arrived at an absurdly large hall already packed full of various dignitaries. From so far back, even standing on tiptoe the Prince couldn't get a decent view of the ruler sitting on his throne at the far end of the hall. All he was able to gather was that the King was extremely pale.

Behind the throne stood eight large men in leather armor, swords at their hips, apparently on the lookout for anything suspicious or out of the ordinary. According to Meng, these men were the Royal Wing—the King's personal guards. Seated comfortably at the King's right hand was a stout elderly man, his beard and clothing styled in the Tang fashion. This man was a prime minister of sorts, whose present duty was to act as regent to the young monarch. Meng continued to recite the name and position of virtually every other person in attendance, but the Prince had no interest in this aristocratic who's who; all the information that Meng relayed to the Prince simply went in one ear and out the other.

The moment the two left the crowded hall, Meng could barely suppress his excitement.

"Well? How did you find the King?"

Unsure what to say, the Prince answered:

"It was hard to get a good look from so far away, but my impression was that he's very pale . . ."

Meng lowered his voice:

"Lately there have been rumors that the King has gone a bit mad. While he's always been pale, I suspect his current pallor has something to do with this development. Whatever the case, his condition may work in our favor when it comes to the matter of saving the girl. The King is secretly desperate to act as a proper Buddhist ruler. He's only waiting for the appropriate moment to show mercy. I imagine he will jump at the prospect. This is not an opportunity to miss."

The Prince couldn't help wondering about Meng's motives. Why was he egging him on in this way? At the same time, the Prince had never been one to care about such mundane matters. It did occur to him that Meng might have been in love with the dancing girl, but he didn't give it much thought, concluding that such things were none of his business.

Several days passed, and the Prince had nothing to do but sit on his hands. Finally, Meng showed up, panting for breath:

"Now's your chance. The King is alone in the Royal Gallery. Will you speak to him?"

Following Meng's instructions, the Prince walked down a long corridor lined with circular windows overlooking the glowing lake, but when he arrived in the gallery, he found no one there—only an assortment of bizarre items that demanded his attention.

There was a large square rack with bronze bells of all sizes that could easily have been mistaken for an instrument of torture; a metallophone with rectangular plates of steel; a sounding stone; and a suspended triangle made of rock or gemstone. They were all musical instruments, but as they appeared to be either heavy stone or metal, the Prince could only imagine that the sounds they made would tear right through a person's soul.

Still more instruments lined the gallery: drums, zithers, flutes, and panpipes. The Prince also found a machine hidden under layers of dust that appeared to be a piece of equipment for observing heavenly bodies—maybe an old south-pointing carriage with a wooden figure on top.

On the walls were portraits of all the Nanzhao kings, beginning with the first, all hanging at the same height. Each of the silk canvases featured a bearded royal with a crown resting on his head. For whatever reason, the image of King Shilong alone was damaged beyond recognition. The Prince had the impression that the damage had been recently inflicted. Then a thought crossed his mind: What if, in a fit of madness, the King had disfigured his own image?

As he stood lost in thought before the ruined portrait, the Prince heard footsteps behind him, then a pale face appeared out of nowhere. There was no doubt it was the King himself. His face bore the timorous look of some sort of rodent, but there was something obsessive—a clear longing—in his eyes. The moment the Prince saw him, he felt an incredible sadness for the young ruler.

As the King stared straight into the Prince's eyes, his expression transformed completely into one of unadulterated happiness. The King exclaimed:

"Master Fuju! You've come at last! I knew you wouldn't forget your promise. Oh, you've come at last!"

The King appeared to be shedding tears of joy, but the Prince stood there stunned, unsure how to respond. The Prince was not well versed in Daoist literature, so he had never heard of this Fuju character. In fact, if by chance he had read *The Lives of the Immortals*, the Prince would probably have been even more baffled to be addressed in this way. As he stood there, unable to produce any kind of reply, the King turned around and screeched:

"Mother! Mother!"

Summoned in this way, Shilong's mother entered the gallery.

Dressed from head to toe in flowing black robes and cutting a majestic figure, she looked to be not a day over forty. The sudden emergence of a third player in this strange scene left the Prince feeling woefully out of his element. Then, recalling that this woman was believed to have been touched by a dragon while bathing in Lake Er, he felt something akin to awe come over him. The King's mother paid no mind to the Prince, giving him only the faintest nod before rushing to her son's side. The King spoke to her:

"Rejoice, Mother! Master Fuju has finally come. I told you about him. . . . I met the Master when I was in Chengdu, remember? His prowess is unmatched in the art of polishing mirrors, and he knows all there is to know about disorders of the mind, so all shall be well! My troubled nature will be put right by the Master. How happy I—"

At this point, the King suddenly dropped to his knees from sheer excitement, then fell face down on the floor. He must have fainted.

The Queen Mother did not seem particularly panicked, so the Prince assumed this was a relatively common occurrence. Standing over her unconscious son, she frowned and said:

"How unfortunate . . ."

Now for the first time, she gave the Prince a proper look and continued:

"I don't know who you are, but if my son is convinced you're Master Fuju, then I would appreciate it if—for his sake— you would do your best to play the part. Agreed?"

"Agreed."

An affirmative answer escaped the Prince's lips, though he could hardly hide his doubts concerning this plan. The Queen Mother sensed his hesitation, of course, and perhaps in an attempt to explain the situation, she said:

"The root of my son's condition is over this way."

Leading him to a corner of the gallery, the Queen Mother removed the cloths draped over a pair of objects—twin mirrors made of nickel, both thirty centimeters in diameter, resting atop wooden stands about a meter apart.

"These mirrors came to us from Chang'an about two hundred years ago as part of the trousseau of a Tang princess. I can't say when it began, but they've become the source of my son's deepest fears. When he looks into them, he sees two of himself. It terrifies him, yet he says he cannot look away. Lately, when he looks into the mirror, he says his reflection comes right out of the mirror and stands there in front of him before vanishing like smoke. He'll stand between the mirrors and watch his reflections multiply and multiply. I've seen him do it. He'll sneak in and spend the whole day in mad communion with his own image . . ."

When the Queen Mother paused, the Prince felt the time was right to ask the question that had been on his mind:

"The King called me Master Fuju, but who is this person?"

"When my son stayed in Chengdu several years ago, he met a Daoist master by that name. My son, you see, is quite convinced that the Master's magic would put an end to the legion of reflections spilling forth from the mirrors."

As the Queen Mother spoke, her son regained consciousness and staggered to his feet. Noticing that the mirrors had been unveiled, he darted toward them and said:

"Take a look, Master! See? My reflection has come out again! Standing right there! Oh, he vanished. Now he's on the other side! The stubborn imp! What can you do to bring an end to this?"

The King looked like a man possessed. His eyes were terribly bloodshot. He stood between the two mirrors, flailing about like a marionette. The Queen Mother could hardly watch. She turned to the Prince and said:

"It's always like this, Master. Please, do something."

But what could he do? After all, the Prince was no Master Fuju. He knew no special tricks. He stood in silence for a moment, staring at the King as he thrashed about madly. Then an idea popped into his head. Who could say if it would work? It was a gamble, but the Prince had to try.

Grabbing the now-exhausted King by his arm, the Prince drew him gently forward.

"Your Majesty, I will perform a sealing spell on the mirrors. If you would be so kind as to watch from here . . . Are you ready?"

Standing the King to one side, the Prince stepped forward, positioning himself right between the mirrors. Then he turned to look into one—would his reflection show or not? As he had suspected, there was nothing there. Just like the lake on the day of his arrival. This only confirmed the Prince's suspicion: He no longer had a reflection. Yet he displayed no dismay, staying within the confident character of the talented Master Fuju. The Prince continued his performance.

"There you have it, Majesty. As you can see, no reflection comes from the mirror. It's sealed inside!"

Peering in from the side, the amazed King saw that, indeed, there was no reflection at all. He stared, mouth agape, overwhelmed by what he had just witnessed.

Then the Prince took the mirrors from their stands, setting them face-to-face against one another.

"Presto! Now the reflections are sealed inside, never again to enter our world. Deprived of light, they shall die in darkness. Milady, please excuse my asking, but might I trouble you for a length of rope? We'll need to bind these mirrors."

As the Prince tied the mirrors together, the King's pale face started to show signs of relief. A long-lost sense of peace seemed to return to him. The King turned back to his mother and said in a shaking voice:

"See, Mother. I told you he was Master Fuju, didn't I?"

ABOUT TEN DAYS LATER, the Prince and Harumaru left Nanzhao on horseback. They followed the Shweli, a tributary of the Irrawaddy, taking the mountain roads from Yunnan to Burma.

Once the Prince had performed his magic on the mirrors, both the King and the Queen Mother had become wholly smitten with him, so the Prince's petition to reduce Harumaru's sentence and have her released into his custody met with no resistance whatsoever. The King begged the Prince to stay, saying his happiness would know no bounds if he could have so moral and erudite a scholar residing within his kingdom, but he would not stand in the way of the Prince's wish to travel to Hindustan.

The King even bestowed upon the Prince two of Yunnan's finest stallions, famed for their endurance. He knew the Prince's journey over the mountains back to Arakan would be a long one, and these steeds would be of no small benefit. The Prince expressed his heartfelt thanks and accepted the kind gift.

The Prince remarked to his young companion as they rode:

"Aren't you glad you've managed to keep your ears?"

"All thanks to you, Miko."

Harumaru had already advanced quite a bit linguistically, so such simple everyday exchanges presented her with no difficulty. Now that she was acting as the Prince's page, she no longer wore her bird wings, instead dressing in the style of a boy.

"Farewell, land of serenity. Farewell, land of peace. Farewell, land of death."

The Prince whispered these words out loud as he finally left Nanzhao with Harumaru at his side. Although he could not say why, his heart was filled with sadness.

For ages, the mountain route running along the Shweli had been well traveled by traders. While the place was famous for the beauty of its rivers and valleys, it was nonetheless a dangerous stretch of land for inexperienced travelers. Its dense forests teemed with all manner of beasts. The insufficiently vigilant also ran the risk of being attacked by fierce barbarians. Though a part of the Southern Lands, the mountainous path reached altitudes of three thousand meters, so some thought had to be given as to how to cope with the unforgiving cold. There was also the risk of tumbling down the steep cliffs on one's horse. Myriad dangers awaited all who traversed these treacherous heights.

The Prince, who was a skilled flutist by all accounts, played "Return to the Castle" as the two proceeded. The flute he played was one that the King of Nanzhao had only recently acquired, and he had given it to the Prince as a parting gift. "Return to the Castle" was thought to repel snakes and, while the Prince didn't necessarily believe in the power of the melody, he couldn't suppress his desire to pull out his flute and play the familiar tune.

One day when the sun was setting and the western sky beyond the mountains had turned deep crimson, the Prince began to feel despondent. He stopped playing his flute, and the whole scene fell into silence. Although not at all predisposed to such feelings, the Prince felt a terrible loneliness fall over him. Was it simply the loneliness of the place? Or was this something that had sprung up within his own heart? As he considered these questions, he saw two riders approaching on horseback.

With the evening sun at their backs, the riders' faces were impossible to see. In shadow, ever nearer the riders came. Finally, the two sets of travelers passed each other. In that instant, out of the corner of his eye, the Prince could see that these two travelers were in every way identical to Harumaru and himself—down to their belongings and the clothes on their backs. The pairs were perfect doubles in every way. The encounter gave the Prince a terrible start, but he let the riders pass with a straight face. Then, the moment they did, he turned around for a second look. But the riders, as well as their horses, had already vanished like smoke.

"Harumaru, did you see that?"

"See what?"

Her calm response made it clear that Harumaru hadn't seen anything at all.

The famed Yunnan stallions ran with supernal speed across miles of mountains, from Lake Er to the Arakan coast. It took only a month for the Prince and Harumaru to arrive where the others were waiting.

When they appeared, Anten jumped out.

"Well, well! Welcome back! And I see the troublemaker is with you. I was wondering where you'd run off to, Akimaru! But here you are, riding up with the Prince as if that were the plan all along. Good grief, child, you don't know the worry you've put us through!"

Anten had apparently mistaken Harumaru for Akimaru. So, with a grin on his face, the Prince explained everything, leaving Anten speechless. Finally, he said:

"How strange. That means Akimaru's really gone. She left ten days ago—and we've not seen hide nor hair of her since."

Now it was the Prince who was lost for words. What could have possessed Akimaru to run off like that without saying anything to him? No matter how long the Prince and the others waited, Akimaru never returned. It seemed that the appearance of Harumaru had coincided with the disappearance of Akimaru. Akimaru must have been reborn as Harumaru in the cave at the foot of Mount Cock-Claw—what other explanation could there be?

PEARL

The thought of death was like an aerial root, finding purchase on a wall and burrowing into it, cracking it open little by little. It all began when the Prince looked upon the shimmering surface of Lake Er and found his own reflection missing. "They say if you look into the water and see no reflection, you will die within the year." The words of that Nanzhao official—Meng, or whatever his name had been—echoed in the Prince's ear. Still, what haunted the Prince was only a thought. He didn't feel any weaker, physically or mentally. On the contrary, he had nothing but confidence in his health. However, the Prince was now a few short years away from celebrating his seventieth birthday. At that age, death could hardly come as a surprise. Emperor Heizei, the Prince's father, had died at forty-nine. His uncle, Emperor Saga, passed away at fifty-five. Even Kūkai entered into nirvana at the age of sixty, didn't he? Thinking in this way, the Prince began to suspect that he might have lived too long already. Yes, it would be tragic for his life to come to an end when Hindustan was so near, but, if that was his fate, so be it.

"I have a feeling, Anten, that I am going to die before long."

The Prince was smiling, but Anten knit his bushy brow, finding the Prince's comment not the least bit funny.

"You mustn't say such ominous things, Miko, especially when Hindustan is right before us. Clearly, you aren't feeling yourself . . ."

The Prince waved Anten's words away with a flick of his wrist.

"No, no. That isn't it at all. I want nothing more than to see Hindustan with my own eyes. That hasn't changed. Yet, as you're aware, the high priests of old all knew when they were going to die. Of course, I lack the proper training, so I have only this vague feeling. I cannot say for certain when the moment will come, but I'm past sixty-five now . . ."

"Sixty-five or seventy-five, why should that make a whit of difference? You shall always be young, Miko. Your youth is what makes you who you are. Were it not so, what would that mean for the rest of us, who look upon you as our Prince?"

"A Prince must be always young? Is that your argument? How absurd! What nonsense! No matter who or what I am, no one can stay young forever."

So the Prince responded, but he hardly had the feeble form of a man approaching seventy. He appeared to be in his mid-fifties at the very oldest. As the Prince spoke with Anten, he strode around the ship with such vigor that no one who saw him would ever imagine that he might be destined to die within a year.

At this moment, the Prince and the others were sailing south through the Bay of Bengal with the monsoon winds at their back. After some time in Arakan, they had found an Arab merchant vessel bound for the Land of Lions: Sinhala. According to legend, the Buddha visited Sinhala three times during his life. As it was only a stone's throw from Hindustan, the travelers now felt quite close to their ultimate destination, and they were sorely tempted to breathe a sigh of relief. Yet, as they had already learned in the past, voyages at sea were anything but predictable.

As they headed for Sinhala, they knew that a safe journey across the bay was by no means guaranteed. At the very least, they would have to pray to the Bodhisattva of Mercy for guidance—and pray they did.

This ship was the kind known to the Tang as an Arabian. It was significantly smaller than the typical Tang vessel, yet surely seaworthy. Its distinctive prow looked durable enough to tame even the wild waves known to rage in the Bay of Bengal. It had a towering aftcastle and boasted four masts in all, including a main mast fitted with a triangular fore-and-aft sail. These features gave the ship an appearance altogether unlike those to which the Prince had become accustomed. Although the ship was an Arab design, it was crewed by a mix of Arabian, Persian, and Indian sailors. Enchanted by the abundant exotica now surrounding him, the Prince ran around the ship as wide-eyed as a child, then reported back to Anten and Engaku everything he had discovered.

One night when the Prince was unable to sleep, he headed topside, where he found the deck bathed in moonlight. Looking up at the aftcastle, the Prince spotted a silhouette. It was a man, staring at a corner of the night sky. He was holding a heavy-looking metal disk at eye level with his right hand as he manipulated the device with his left. For some time, the Prince watched from below as the man went about his work. Soon, however, he could no longer contain his curiosity, and he addressed the man:

"Say, what is it you're doing up there?"

Glancing down at the Prince for only a moment, the man replied:

"Measuring the elevation of the stars."

"The stars?"

"Aye. The Northern Dragon and the Gilded Canopy, to be precise. It's my measurements that keep us on our course for Sinhala—I hold us five and a half fingers from the Twins in the Canopy. Not to brag, but I'm the only man on the ship who can work the astrolabe."

Even as the man uttered these puzzling words, his eyes never left the sky. The Prince was all the more curious now, and he asked:

"Do you mind if I come up?"

"Be my guest."

Climbing the narrow ladder, the Prince found that the man with the astrolabe was surprisingly young. As the Prince soon learned, though the man spoke the Tang language as well as anyone, he had been born in the Persian capital of Isfahan. From there, he made his way to Baghdad to study astronomy. Completing his studies, he put his knowledge of the stars to use and became the navigator for this ship. Through his various travels east and west, the man had acquired an encyclopedic knowledge well beyond his years. He apparently had an unfaltering command of not only Tang but several other languages as well.

This man, whose name was Kamal, astonished the Prince with the breadth of his knowledge. In turn, the Prince's noble upbringing and courteous manner seemed to leave an impression on the young astronomer. The two passed the whole night in friendly conversation. Before they knew it, a pale light appeared in the sky to the east.

Glancing down at the water, the Prince thought he saw a creature kicking up white waves, and he squinted to get a better look. He was sure the thing wasn't human, but its round, smooth head was hardly piscine. The animal would disappear beneath the surface, only to bob up again for air some time later. The Prince leaned over the side, then turned to ask his companion:

"Did you see that thing swimming there?"

"What's that?"

The Prince pointed downward, and Kamal looked at the water for a second or two, but quickly returned his gaze to the sky. Here was a man completely uninterested in marine matters.

"I must confess. I have no affinity at all for the ocean. My calling is in the stars and the stars alone. For me, a star in flight is an event as important as the collapse of a great nation. And yet I would not so much as blink if a throng of sea monsters suddenly appeared before me."

Kamal laughed at himself. The Prince smiled and laughed along.

Soon enough, the creature vanished from sight—only to resurface later that same day. The Prince was leaning against the stern ladder, playing a tune on the ancient flute he had received from King Shilong, when a spot in the sea began bubbling up. Then, perhaps in response to the Prince's melody, the animal popped its head out of the water. As this had happened before, the Prince was not in the least shocked. Harumaru happened to be standing nearby, so the Prince called her over. But for the young girl from Yunnan, for whom the ocean itself was still something new, this animal was all too frightening.

"What is that, that loathsome thing! It looks just like a person!"

Seeing Harumaru's reaction, the Prince stepped in between the frightened girl and the bulwark, as if to protect her from the sight.

"Come now, there's nothing to fear. I've come across such a creature before. Where was it—not far from Guangzhou? As I recall, the locals called it a dugong or something like that. It's a clever animal, I've learned. It's even capable of picking up human language. Nothing scary about—"

But before the Prince could finish reassuring the child, the dugong rose chest-high out of the water and looked Harumaru in the eye. Then the animal spoke in clear human words:

"Wonderful to see you again, my dearest Akimaru! Don't tell me you don't remember me!"

Harumaru would surely have been scared witless by the sea beast's gaze alone, but now it *spoke* to her! With that, she turned white as a sheet. It looked as though she was going to pass out then and there. Indifferent to the effect it had had on Harumaru, the dugong continued:

"I remember it all, Akimaru. You were the one who taught me to use words, and never for a moment have I forgotten your kindness. It was the language you gave me that allowed me to return to life after my death in that suffocating southern jungle. But why explain such things to you? You already know all this, don't you, Akimaru?"

The Prince could no longer stand by and watch as the animal spoke to Harumaru in this way. He cut in:

"Dugong! The child you see before you is not Akimaru, though the resemblance is admittedly uncanny. This is Harumaru of the mountains of Yunnan, a child unaccustomed to sea creatures of your kind. In fact, she seems to be terrified, so how about leaving her be? I beg you, on her behalf . . ."

The dugong stared at Harumaru for some time before finally withdrawing in silence.

Harumaru continued shaking uncontrollably, even after the dugong was out of sight. The Prince did his best to calm her down.

"What could be so terrifying? It's only an animal. . . ."

"Never in my life have I seen an animal that looks so human. Ever since I was a little girl, I have been very fond of Lake Er and the fish that live in it, but nothing nearly as strange as this dugong creature abides there! And then there's what it said. Did it not say it had died in some jungle somewhere? Doesn't that make it not a dugong but the ghost of a dugong?"

"I don't know if I can answer that question, Harumaru . . ."

"There's still more that terrifies me, Miko."

"Indeed?"

"Yes. I don't know this Akimaru of whom the creature spoke. Still, I can't help feeling as though, in another life, I might have met this dugong—"

"What are you saying? Moments ago, you told me you'd never seen such a creature."

"No, I said 'never in my life.' But before I was born ..."

"Before you were born?"

"Perhaps the dugong is right. Perhaps we did know each other. In fact, I might have been the one who taught the animal to speak. Could it be a memory from a past life? Or maybe some sort of illusion? Please, Miko, if you have any thoughts on the matter, do enlighten me."

The Prince wished he could say something comforting to Harumaru, but he could make no more sense of these strange happenings than she could.

THE ARABIAN SCUDDED ACROSS the raging waves of the Bay of Bengal as it made a beeline south. The sun was burning like a ball of fire overhead, the sea nearly boiling over. Unable to bear the extreme heat, the sailors stripped down to their loincloths. Now only the Prince and Harumaru remained decently dressed. Since the crew believed Harumaru to be a young man, they openly mocked her "boyish bashfulness."

When night fell, Kamal climbed up the aftcastle ladder, as was his habit, to navigate by the stars. The sky was full of them— but, as the ship advanced toward the equator, Polaris came to hover just above the horizon, rendering Kamal's precious astrolabe entirely useless. He now relied solely on the Twins. Kamal was able to calculate their distance from Sinhala by the positions of these stars—these stars that never strayed. By their light, Kamal could see that the vessel was presently four or five days away from dropping anchor in the port of Trincomalee. Thus proving his talents as a navigator, Kamal broke into a grin, his white teeth shining in the starlight.

The land of Sinhala is known in Book Six of Pliny the Elder's *Natural History* as Taprobane. According to Pliny, Taprobane had long been viewed as the Antipodes: the opposite end of the world. At that time, it was believed to stretch from the northern hemisphere down into the southern. In fact, the knowledge that Sinhala was an island and not a continent came only in the age of Alexander the Great. We can see that Pliny had no small interest in this place as in Book Nine he returns to Taprobane, remarking on its role as one of the world's foremost producers of pearls. Pliny's *History* was seldom accurate, but this statement was true, it turns out. Sinhala produced pearls of extraordinary size and quality. When discussing "world-famous pearls," one most likely thinks of the Hainanese shores of Hepu, known since the Han dynasty, yet Sinhala was no less distinguished in this regard, as we can see from Faxian's *Record of Buddhist Lands,* in which it is mentioned as a major producer of "pearls and myriad other treasures." The island also appears in the *Christian Topography* of Cosmas Indicopleustes, so we can see that, from as early as the sixth century, Sinhala was a first-class entrepôt where all sorts of goods—including silk, aloeswood, sandalwood, and pearls—were traded in great quantities.

One morning, when the Prince was strolling along the deck with Anten, Engaku, and Harumaru, the image of an island-like mass appeared on the horizon on the starboard side. Anten immediately lit up in anticipation.

"Ah! Now it is only a dot, but is that not Sinhala? If so, then everything we have endured will not have been in vain! Oh, happy day!"

Engaku tried to temper Anten's gleeful expectations.

"It's too early to say for certain. Though that may look like land, it's far too small to be the Land of Lions. It could well be a pod of whales or some stretch of reef. Best not to get ahead of ourselves . . ."

His happy moment ruined in this way, Anten replied:

"Engaku, why must you always spoil everything?"

Yet, when the ship drew closer, it was just as Engaku had said. Far from being Sinhala, what had appeared to be a land mass was only a minor cluster of reefs jutting out of the water. There were men there, too—at least a dozen of them, presumably Kunlun. Some lay on the rocks half-naked while others waded in the shoals, their dark skin glistening in the scorching sun. Those in the water were completely naked, swimming about without a shred of shame. Some of them spotted the ship and waved amiably. The men were yelling, but the Prince and his companions couldn't understand what they were saying. Then Kamal appeared on the deck, proving his worth not only as a navigator but as an interpreter as well. He spoke for some time with the man who appeared to be their chief, then turned toward the Prince and explained:

"These men are pearl divers. Diving, as far as I can tell, is strictly controlled by the state of Sinhala. Citizens are forbidden from taking part, which means these men are either authorized by the government or they're poachers—I haven't asked. Whatever the case, it would surely be worthwhile to watch them dive. What do you think, shall we ask them to show us how they do it?"

The long voyage had left every soul on the ship suffering from boredom, so none opposed Kamal's suggestion. They asked the captain to keep the ship steady for a short while.

When Kamal explained everything to the diver chief, a devilish smile spread across his face. His mouth was blood red, presumably from betel nut. He turned around and asked something of his men.

Right away, a canoe slid out from behind some nearby rocks and three men climbed in. Once they had paddled out to deeper waters, they jumped out of the boat one after the other. It was then that the Prince noticed the divers were carrying objects resembling long trumpets or bull's horns—gently curved and darkly shining.

From the deck of the ship, the Prince and the others looked on in disbelief. Their eyes were set on the spot where the men dove in, but ten minutes passed, then twenty, and still there was no sign of them. Time went on, but not so much as the slightest eddy or bubble formed on the water. Finally out of patience, the Prince turned to Engaku and said:

"Incredible! Can these men really hold their breath so long?"

With a smug look on his face, Engaku replied:

"Did you not see what they had in their hands, that thing that looked like the horn of a bull? That's the trick. From what I could see, it was likely rhinoceros horn."

"Rhinoceros horn!"

Engaku wiggled his nose triumphantly.

"It's all but unknown in our native land, but there is a piece of Daoist literature that is well known in Tang: *The Master Who Embraces Simplicity*. According to this text, there is an animal known as the heavenly horn rhinoceros. Its horn, which can measure thirty centimeters in length, features a distinctive white stripe. Now, if one carves this horn into the shape of a fish, then dives into the water holding one end to their mouth, they will find the water no different from the air. It would seem that these pearl divers have taken advantage of this old Daoist secret. At any rate, it was probably this rhinoceros horn that they held in their hands. Nay, I am certain of it."

"Rhinoceros horn, you say. I find it hard to accept, but, having seen with my own eyes how long the men have been underwater, I suppose I have no choice but to take you at your word."

When forty or so minutes had passed, the water finally began to bubble. All watched as the men surfaced with those black horns pressed to their mouths like trumpets. As they lowered the horns, the divers smiled dazzlingly. No, it was not their teeth that shone. The men had stored the pearls in their cheeks, and now the bright spheres appeared even whiter inside their betel-red mouths.

Inspecting the pearls, the diver chief carefully chose the largest and finest from the haul, surely hoping that presenting it to the Prince would lead to a handsome reward. As the Prince had always had a penchant for precious gems, he happily received the chief's pearl. It was large, probably over a centimeter in diameter—and almost perfectly spherical. It had a blue shine to it. . . . No, in a different light, it had a pale and dewy pink color.

The Prince rolled the pearl around in the palm of his hand, admiring its kaleidoscopic hues.

"To think nature could produce so beautiful an object. . . . Fantastic, isn't it?"

As he was wont to do, Engaku interrupted:

"Pardon my saying so, Miko, but I can't shake the feeling that such beautiful objects tend to bode ill."

At this, Anten added sarcastically:

"And how's the view from your horse, sir?"

Engaku paid no attention to Anten, as if his mockery was nothing but the sound of the wind.

"In the well-known Daoist work *Huainanzi*, there is a chapter entitled 'Forest of Persuasions,' which contains a passage that goes something like this: 'The moon-bright pearl is the oyster's malady but my profit. Tiger claws and elephant tusks do the animals benefit, but they do me harm.' What captures our eyes, this beauty, is no more than an irritation to the shellfish itself. This is what makes the pearl. We must not forget that Devaputra Māra attempted to sway Śākyamuni with temptresses who concealed their twisted nature beneath beautiful appearances. Who can say if beautiful things are beautiful because they are twisted, or if they are twisted because they are beautiful? What we can say for certain is that the two phenomena are closely linked. Personally, I am wary of any beautiful object, be it a woman, a flower, or a piece of pottery. Seeing Miko holding this pearl, I cannot help but fear that, in the future, this object will bring untold misfortune. Then again, I have a habit of borrowing trouble. While it may seem that I'm disagreeing with you, Miko, please know that I mean nothing else by it."

As the Prince listened to Engaku pontificate in this way, what began to percolate in his heart, rising to the surface like marsh gas bubbles, was the thought of death—a thought he had managed to put out of his mind for some time. "They say if you look into the water and and see no reflection, you will die within the year." That voice rang again in his ears, seemingly floating on the ocean wind, and it left him stunned. If, as Engaku feared, this pearl augured ill, what was keeping the Prince from simply hurling the thing into the sea? It had already been revealed to the Prince that he would die within the year, even though he had yet to realize his lifelong dream of traveling to Hindustan. It would surely be prudent of the Prince to keep a good distance from anything that might bring ill fortune. But the exact opposite thought could be found in the Prince's mind as well. To wit: Since he was already fated to die, what was left to fear? Why should he not indulge in the beauties of the world to whatever extent possible? The Prince was so fond of treasures such as this one. Engaku stated his case as best he could, but, having been given a pearl of such rare quality, the Prince could not imagine why he should discard it as if it had been a piece of trash.

Then, as if to clear the air of such grave talk, Anten's laughter resounded from the deck.

"Pearls of wisdom, indeed! Morality tales of Śākyamuni and Māra! Really, Engaku, I never pegged you as a sermonizer. Pearls and demonic seductresses! Beauty and affliction! Then let me ask: The Prince has a beautiful soul, does he not? Does that mean his soul is twisted? Is that how you see it?"

"No, that's not what I meant. But we can see in scripture that outward beauty is not necessarily something to be trusted—"

High-handedly, Anten now cut Engaku off mid-speech:

"Let me tell you how I see it: Yes, the Prince's soul and the pearl are one and the same. There's no need to distinguish between different types of beauty. Moreover, if beauty is a byproduct of affliction, what's wrong with that? If you think about it, there's no reason not to call the Prince's fondness for pearls—pardon my saying so—an illness of the mind. But if that's so, it's his mind that has brought this pearl into the world, is it not? That, in short, is why they are linked. I don't think, as you apparently do, that we must view this connection between beauty and affliction in such a negative light."

Verbal sparring of this kind might seem hostile, but Anten

and Engaku were always engaging in these heated debates. For the two monks, it was little more than a game—a sport. Though he was at the center of this war of words, the Prince listened in amusement as the monks fired back and forth. While the thought of death was certainly on his mind, it wasn't something that filled him with dread or fear, only a vague anticipation—as if it were something he was looking forward to, a new adventure. The Prince thought, perhaps I have called this pearl into existence, as Anten suggested, and now I hold it in my hand as a manifestation of the death that awaits me.

The diver chief received a generous reward for the pearl and then departed with a bright-red grin. Presently, the ship weighed anchor and set sail once more.

Shortly after their departure, Harumaru—where had she been?—appeared at the Prince's side, cowering in fear. She said in a shaky voice:

"Have the pearl divers gone? Their chief frightened me, so I hid below. That plump man looked just like a dugong! Right down to his bald head."

The Prince cracked a wry smile and said:

"What a strange child you are. First you see a dugong so man-like it scares you half to death; now you see a man so dugong-like you scamper off and hide in fear! His skin may have been darker than yours or mine, but there was nothing out of the ordinary about him. Or maybe, in your eyes, he was a dugong in human form?"

While there seem to be no stories of dugongs taking human form, there are Tang tales about shark people. These stories need not be recounted here in full, but legend has it that when these shark people cried, pearls would stream from their eyes. Sometimes a shark person would assume human form and visit the home of a person nearby. If the host showed their guest kindness, then the shark person would leave behind pearly tears as tokens of their gratitude. Of course, the Prince was not as versed in the Tang classics as Engaku, so there was little chance he had ever heard of these beings, but as he spoke with Harumaru, what he saw in his mind's eye was not so different from this mythical creature. Indeed, as Harumaru said, the chubby diver chief looked very much like a dugong. Maybe he had in fact been a dugong, passing for a man! So the Prince told himself, although he said not a word about it to Harumaru.

SOON AFTER THAT, THE crew began noticing strange phenomena.

According to Kamal, they ought to have reached the northern shore of Sinhala within days. Yet—had the trustworthy stars gone suddenly mad?—they had not arrived as he had predicted. Some ten days had passed, and the ship remained at sea, with no sign of land on the horizon. Betrayed by his own tools, Kamal sat on the deck all night, his pride deeply wounded, trying to decipher the star-filled sky with bloodshot eyes. The sky was ablur, its many stars appearing to double. Meteors shot by in vast numbers, boggling the young man's mind. In frustration, he soon began to tear the hair from his head.

Nor were the odd occurrences limited to the night sky above. They could be found on the water as well. This wasn't the first time the ship found itself enveloped in fog—a fog so thick that it was as dim as twilight, even at midday—but unlike such moments in the past, the ship could not push through this foggy barrier. Behind each layer of fog lay another. Unable to escape, the ship sailed cautiously onward, meandering slowly as if making its way through some sort of labyrinth. The Arab captain found this lack of progress so exasperating that he soon stopped barking commands at his crew altogether. He now confined himself to his cabin, where he sulked and slept for days on end.

It was not long before strange forces started to affect the members of the crew as well.

One maddeningly hot night, the men were sitting on deck half-naked. Lacking even the slightest breeze to cool them, they sweated profusely. There was nothing for them to do but turn to strong drink and boisterous song. Almost as if some invisible power was driving them on, the men lost themselves to wailing; perhaps they were voicing their deepest and darkest anxieties in the form of song. As ever, the Prince stood at the stern ladder, half-watching the gloomy, drunken spectacle.

Within an hour, the men who had been belting out shanties had all fallen silent as if they'd suddenly sobered up. They remained cross-legged on the deck, but—perhaps overcome by sleep—they were now rocking gently back and forth. Abruptly, one of the young sailors rose to his feet and went over to the side of the ship, presumably to take in the night sea. The other men watched languidly. After a moment or two, the sailor turned back to look at them and gave a big grin. Seeing this, the others in the circle smiled back. It was then that the smiling sailor pulled off his loincloth and, for reasons unknown, leapt naked into the ocean below.

He was the first, but not the last, to go overboard that night. Only fifteen minutes later, one of the others stood up silently and staggered toward the edge before tossing himself into the sea.

The third man to plunge into the night sea was somewhat different from the other two. First, he let out a giant yawn, rubbed his eyes, and got up to stroll around the deck. Then, as if the thought had just occurred to him, he walked over to the Prince at the ladder and tapped him on the shoulder:

"Meeko, I don't think I can take much more of this. How about a pick-me-up tune on your flute?"

The Arab sailors tended to elongate the first vowel when they called the Prince "Miko."

When the sailor put his hand on his shoulder, the Prince felt as though he had just awoken from a dream. He immediately ran below to fetch his flute, but by the time he returned, the man was gone.

He had already jumped to his death.

The oddest thing about this spate of suicides, however, was that the other men in the circle simply watched, doing nothing to stop it despite being right there. They didn't get up or cry out. They sat there like lumps of stone—and not because they were unwilling to lend a hand. The Prince was equally helpless, the thought of intervening never even crossing his mind. He felt as if he'd been watching some silent play being performed on a distant stage. When the third man to die had tapped him on the shoulder, the Prince recovered some sense of reality. Yet even then, he did nothing to stop the self-destructive sailors. Evidently, a curse had fallen over the ship, stealing the sanity of not only the Prince, but all on board.

Try as the men might to free themselves from the grip of the curse, however, there appeared to be no release from this nightmare. The ship remained exactly where it was. At night, when the heat was at its worst, a handful of sailors would leap to a watery grave. The ship had a crew of about a hundred men, so there was no immediate threat of running short of hands.

The remaining sailors said nothing about what was

happening. Even so, the Prince sternly warned Harumaru against going topside after dark.

Five or so days later, the night brought a light breeze. Life returned to the dead water and ripples formed on its surface. While it wasn't enough to fill the sail, the ship rocked from side to side as if warming up. Figuring this meant that the curse had been lifted at last, the Prince called Harumaru to the deck to feel the evening breeze. At the ladder, the Prince played a tune on the Nanzhao flute for the first time in a long while. The instrument's design was perfectly ordinary, but as it was made with the finest Yunnanese bamboo and ivory, it had gained an amber patina with age.

As the Prince played, a frosty blast sliced through the southern swelter.

After a while, the Prince lowered the flute from his lips. He was in a daze again. There's a saying: Play the flute with spirit, and it might slip out of your mouth as you do. In that moment, the Prince had to wonder if that was what he was experiencing. He could tell that something wasn't right. On the lookout for signs of more trouble, he turned to Harumaru. She was stiff, staring at something on the sea. The Prince was now accustomed to the girl's perpetual skittishness, so he quickly assumed that some insignificant thing had spooked the child yet again. Still, he asked:

"What is it? Do you see something out there?"

Before the Prince could finish his question, Harumaru lifted a shaky finger to point at a distant patch of sea to port. She said in a wavering voice:

"Wh-what is that ship?"

"What?"

Through a gap in the fog, the Prince saw the ship—but

what kind of ship was this? It had arrow slits in the bulwarks, catapults on the deck, and banners of all sizes fluttering among its masts. It looked to be an ancient warship, floating eerily in the distance. The black night had no moon and no stars, but this ship glowed with a pale light, trembling like a reflection in the water. Then the Prince realized: The ghostly vessel was turning slowly, making its way toward them.

As the ship approached, a closer look revealed men, scores of them. . . . But could they really be called men? They had the general shape of people, yes, but their faces and bodies lacked definition. It seemed their shadowy forms might dissolve into the night fog at any moment. They were lined up along the side of the ship, and their eyes—if they even had eyes—appeared to be set on the Arabian. These men, too, seemed to ripple, expanding and contracting like reflections in the water.

"Are those truly men? Living men? I cannot tell . . ."

Perhaps Harumaru didn't hear the Prince's whisper. She remained stiff and silent as she stared at the strange ship.

Before long, the ship was right beside theirs. The two were touching now, but the prow of the approaching ship was much lower than their own. Even though ship had hit ship, it was as if the smaller vessel weighed nothing at all. By that time, the shadow-men had already tossed grappling hooks onto the deck of the Arabian and rushed up the side in great numbers.

*Hyara hyara hyara hyara hyara hyara*—this otherworldly sound issued ceaselessly from their dark mouths. The men were apparently laughing.

The Prince told Harumaru to run, and the two of them scurried across the deck for cover, but it was already too late. Shadows closed in all around them. There was nowhere for them to hide.

*Hyara hyara hyara hyara hyara hyara.*

The shadow-men cackled as they pawed at the Prince and Harumaru with hands as cold as ice water. Their probing fingers left the Prince's skin damp and covered in goosebumps. Harumaru looked just like a frightened opossum, letting the shadow-men do as they would. Likewise, the Prince didn't resist, realizing that no good could come from opposing the invaders.

The men groped every inch of the Prince's person with their frigid hands. They first grabbed the flute he had in his right hand, then took the tiger-skin flint pouch from his waist. The pearl the diver chief had given the Prince was in that bag, and when they snatched it from him, the Prince flew into a rage, staging a desperate fight against the thieves.

Why did the Prince feel the need to fight for the pearl? Engaku had expounded at some length on the dangers the pearl posed—then again, Anten had tried to refute him, even going so far as to suggest that the pearl was a psychic extension of the Prince himself. Whatever the case, the Prince had become dearly attached. Cursed or not, he thought, the pearl and I are inextricably linked. How could I stand by and watch them take it from me? The Prince boldly threw off the shadow-men with all his might, made a fist, and punched hard at the chest of the nearest man. Yet he found no substance there to catch his blow—they were truly only shadows.

In the struggle, the well-worn sack ripped open, and the pearl flew out. It nearly rolled off the deck, but the Prince grabbed it in the nick of time. Immediately, two or three shadowy hands rushed toward him, but he was completely unwilling to part with the pearl, so he put it in his mouth and swallowed it. No one could take it from him now.

Instantly, the Prince's head started to spin, and he passed

out. As he lost consciousness, the only thing he heard was the hollow laughter of the shadow-men all around him.

*Hyara hyara hyara hyara hyara hyara.*

WHEN HE FINALLY WOKE from his long sleep, the first thing the Prince felt was a slight pain, as if something was lodged in his throat. He tried to cough it up, and he tried to gulp it down, but nothing worked. His mouth was painfully dry. He felt around, hoping to find some water.

With his eyes wide open in the total darkness, the Prince tried to pick up the severed thread of his memory. What had become of the pearl? Yes, when the shadow-men attacked, didn't he swallow it to keep it from them? So, was this pain in his throat the pearl? Was such a thing even possible?

When the Prince was a child of about three or so, he happened to swallow a gem no smaller than this one. It probably came from a piece of jewelry belonging to a lady of the Inner Palace. One day, reclining on the slatted veranda overlooking the eastern courtyard of Seiryō-den, the Prince was playing with the precious object when it landed in his mouth. In the moment, he panicked and wound up swallowing it. It slowly passed through his esophagus and into his stomach. This resulted in quite a commotion around the court. A number of famous healers were summoned, but none of their potions or elixirs had any effect on the boy. Finally, Kusuko burst in with a purgative of her own devising and had the stone out of the boy three mornings later, much to the relief of everyone at the court.

Once it was out of him, it was Kusuko who thrust her hand into the chamber pot to retrieve the item from the child's excreta. Finding it, she broke into the most triumphant grin. Even now, the Prince could recall that radiant look of satisfaction on Kusuko's face. The memory brought a smile to his lips. It was almost enough to make the Prince forget the pain in his throat.

Where was the Prince now? He could hardly be on a ship. He felt no swaying, no rising nor falling. Did that mean that the Arab ship had at last escaped the cursed waters and reached its destination of Sinhala? Or had a malevolent wind blown them yet again to some strange and distant island? With no idea where he was, the Prince sat up and cried out:

"Hello! Anybody?"

The Prince heard his own voice but was shocked to find it completely unrecognizable. Nothing came from his mouth but a hoarse, dry rasp. Something was wrong. The Prince had tried to convince himself that the pain wasn't so bad, that it was all in his mind, but that did not appear to be the case. This pain was very real indeed. There was something in his throat. The Prince told himself: If I am in fact bound to die this year, then this will surely be the cause.

With this, the Prince felt as though a great weight had been lifted from his shoulders. The wheels of fate were spinning away in silence, guiding the Prince ever closer to a secret and unknowable end. There was no need for him to spend his energy trying to predict the moment of his coming death as if he were a high priest of old. After all, he told himself, I now hold death inside my throat. I shall make my way to Paradise carrying this pearl of death within me. Then, the moment I arrive at my destination, it will burst open, releasing an indescribable fragrance, and I'll die in rapture! No—wherever I die, wherever I happen to be, that place will be Paradise. Because when this pearl bursts open, its heavenly fragrance shall burst out of me as well. How liberating! Now in the highest of spirits, the Prince called out again:

"Hello! Anten? Engaku? Where are you? If you can hear me, say something!"

But the voice that came from the Prince sounded pitiful—like the sound produced by a cracked flute. It was hard on the ear, a far cry from the voice of a man in excellent health.

What had happened? And where was it that the ship had landed? Where was the Prince? Let us leave these questions unanswered—until the Prince discovers his own whereabouts. For the time being, suffice it to say that it was not his original destination of Sinhala.

# VIŇKĀ

Zhou Qufei was probably the first to write about the Bay of Bengal's so-called wicked waters. The Song-dynasty official was posted to Lingnan and later recorded his observations in ten volumes collectively known as *The Land Beyond the Passes.* According to Zhou, ships leaving Lamuri for Quilon had to exercise extreme caution to avoid a certain stretch of water near Sinhala. Should a ship stray in that direction, he tells us, it would end up sailing in circles eternally, or be slammed by a head-wind so powerful it would find itself thrust back to Lamuri with unearthly speed. Although the outbound journey from Lamuri to the so-called wicked waters required the better part of a month, unfortunate sailors would find themselves carried back to their point of departure in no more than one night. This was no ordinary gust, but just the kind of wind one would expect to encounter over cursed waters. The Prince's ship must have wandered into this patch of sea and ended up swept away.

The Arabian was transported far to the east, arriving at the northern tip of the Isle of Sumatra by dawn, although none on board knew it. In other words, even the talented navigator Kamal had no idea where it was that they had made land.

At the time, there was a kingdom on Sumatra bearing the name Srivijaya—also known to the Tang as Shili Foshi. For some hundred years, it had been acknowledged throughout the region as a land in which Buddhism had reached full flower. While the Golden Age of Srivijaya had already come and gone, a single glance at the glorious stupas of brick and stone that covered the land was enough to see that this realm had been blessed with the light of the Greater Vehicle. Even the forgotten icons and lingams hidden among the trees seemed to join in the joyful chorus. Arriving two hundred years before the Prince, the monk Yijing stayed here for seven and a half years. That is, even in Yijing's time, there was something in this place to hold a monk's attention.

As the sun rose, the Prince and his companions set foot on this strange land for the first time. They could never have dreamed they'd landed in a Buddhist kingdom some hundred li removed from the Bay of Bengal. Taking in the myriad monuments and stupas on every hill and in every valley, stretching up into the sky like pyramids, they had to doubt their eyes. Was this not Hindustan itself? How could it be otherwise? Spotting a particularly grand stupa aglow in red ocher, Anten marveled:

"We have seen Chenla, Panpan, and Arakan—all of which flowered with Buddhism—but never have we encountered such magnificent displays of devotion! Look! This must be Sinhala! Engaku, what do you think?"

Equally excited by what he saw, Engaku exclaimed:

"While I cannot say if it is Sinhala or not, there can be no mistake that we've come very close to Hindustan. This land shines with the light of the Buddha's teachings. Perhaps we've even passed Sinhala and reached Hindustan. Everything around us suggests it. Take the exotic scent wafting in the air—is that only my imagination? I've never experienced anything like it before. Well, Miko, what do you make of this? Where do you think we are?"

Engaku prodded the Prince for an answer, but he remained strangely silent. Engaku was ecstatic at the thought of having arrived in Hindustan, so he found the Prince's reticence vexing.

"Judging from your silence, I assume your throat is worse than it was last night? I feared as much. . . . Unless, of course, there's something else on your mind . . ."

The Prince laughed this away.

"No, nothing of the sort. I simply find it hard to believe

we're as close to Hindustan as you both seem to think. That's all."

This caught Engaku off guard.

"And why is that?"

The Prince squeezed out a hoarse reply:

"Well, think about it. How could we have arrived in Hindustan so easily? I suspect many more obstacles stand between us and our final destination. First and foremost, what kind of hard-fought prize would Hindustan be if all it took was some wind to blow us there?"

Answering in Engaku's place, Anten said in astonishment:

"'So easily'? Miko, we left Guangzhou nearly a year ago, and have spent the intervening months wandering the Southern Lands in vain. If anything, the thought that we still haven't arrived in Hindustan after having endured so much is enough to bring me to tears! I think it's about time we arrived at our goal. 'All it took'? Please, don't be ridiculous! I have to wonder, Miko, if you aren't seeking out unnecessary pain and trouble! If we've arrived in Sinhala, it means that our misadventures are finally over . . . "

"To be sure. If we have indeed arrived in Sinhala. Well, I suppose we shall find out soon enough."

And so the Prince put the pointless debate to rest. Anten and Engaku followed him as he set off toward the hilly interior. It was clear that the Prince was anxious to get a good look at this new land, wherever it happened to be.

The island was certainly different from the Southern Lands that the Prince and the others had seen thus far. It had been formed by a chain of volcanoes; some were active, while others, now dormant, seemed to have erupted without warning in the past, leaving numerous religious structures partially buried.

Walking on, they came across huge mounds of hardened lava, ash, and rock from what could only have been a truly formidable eruption. And yet plants had grown back everywhere, even atop the volcanic ruins, flourishing in the wet climate. The Prince and the others passed through patches of marshland in which the air was oppressively humid, and the thick clusters of ferns all around them threatened to ensnare them in the mire should they venture too close.

After walking about a li, they arrived at a clearing: a nearly circular hollow amid the thick jungle. Toward the middle of the hollow was a pool filled with clear water, and by the edge of the pool—what was this bizarre flower? It looked to be about a meter in diameter and had five massive, unnaturally red petals. Who had ever seen so large and resplendent a flower? Furthermore, it appeared to have no stem at all, nor leaves. In other words, this plant was a flower and nothing else. It was almost as though, entirely unlike any ordinary flower, this blossom had sprung right out of the earth. Yet there it was, reflecting in the water, giving off a blood-red color that showed the travelers that it was very much alive.

Some thousand years after the Prince, an enterprising British official with the East India Company, a man by the name of Thomas Stamford Raffles, led an exploration of Sumatra, where he stumbled across what would come to be known as the world's largest flower. It was later given the name *Rafflesia*, the name by which it is still known today, but the Prince and his fellow monks were distant in every sense from the world to come, so this monstrous flower rang no bells. For all his botanical expertise, Engaku was clueless when it came to the exotic specimens native to these remote lands, which were full of plants that could not be found in the compendiums produced in the Tang empire.

So, the three monks stood there, mouths agape, looking at the flower from a safe distance. Eventually, Anten spoke in a low voice, addressing no one in particular:

"If there were a man who was nothing but a floating head, we would no doubt call him a monster. So this flower, which appears to be nothing but a blossom, must be monstrous as well! The more I look at it, the more it disturbs me. To come across so perverse a plant here surely does suggest that this place is no Sinhala. It seems more like a savage land not yet graced by the Buddha's light. Really, what kind of place is this?"

Then Engaku spoke, as if to himself:

"The Lord Buddha sits on a lotus blossom, yes, but what creature would sit upon so foul a flower? Its shape is closer to the camellia than the lotus. It looks like a giant camellia blossom fallen to the ground. I seem to remember a passage in the *Zhuangzi*, in 'Free and Easy Wandering,' that reads: 'In ancient times, there was a Great Camellia for which eight thousand years passed as a single spring and eight thousand years passed as a single autumn.' But this flower is surely no camellia! It reeks of death, filling my nostrils with its stench even from this distance. I think I'm going to be sick!"

Only the Prince said nothing. It was as if he had forgotten to speak. His eyes couldn't get enough of this incredible flower that repulsed all visitors under the blazing sun.

The three of them were standing there in silence when they felt a presence. Someone spoke to them from behind:

"You people—who are you?"

The travelers turned around to see a young man wearing only a loincloth. He was so skinny that his ribs jutted out. The man's eyes focused on the three monks, probing them. The language he spoke was quite familiar to our travelers, as they had picked it up during their time in Panpan. It was Malay. This being the case, they had no difficulty understanding the man's question. Anten answered:

"Travelers. We've come from Japan."

"This is no place for wandering. What are you doing here?"

"Well, there's the strangest flower just over there, and I suppose we lost track of time staring at it."

The man looked at them suspiciously.

"Now I have to ask: You didn't touch the flower, did you?"

Anten threw his head back and laughed.

"Touch it? Why would anyone ever do such a thing? Even if you begged me, I wouldn't lay a finger on it."

Apparently relieved by Anten's attitude, the man now spoke more softly:

"The plant you saw is a man-eating flower. It will quickly suck a person dry and make a mummy of them. You were wise to stay away from it."

Anten was shocked.

"This is the first I've heard of a man-eating flower. Do you have many of them around here?"

"No, not many. The volcanoes have been relatively quiet recently, and these flowers, which rely on the warmth of the soil, have consequently declined in number. We probably have no more than thirty at present. Still, they are highly valued plants, and that's why I have been appointed flower guard. If they die, I shall lose face—and my job as well."

"What reason could there be to protect such an odd flower? Who has asked you to do this?"

"The King, of course. As for his reasons, the flower is used to preserve the queens of the realm. It serves no other purpose."

Anten was about to ask another question when a trumpet

sounded in the distant valley. At this, the flower guard suddenly became animated.

"Lo! The Queen's procession is returning from the temple. It sounds as though they are heading through the valley now. Go down and see her, if you like. The living queen is a sight we lesser men are not often granted! Her beauty is something you will not want to miss. Hurry! Once the Queen has a child, that rare beauty will never again be seen! Go now, go!"

Although unsure why they were doing it, the three of them rushed down the hill as urged by the guard. They finally came to the bottom of the green valley and hid in the shade of a large tree, waiting to catch a glimpse of the Queen.

Before long, a procession arrived, but with little of the pomp and circumstance typically associated with the word. There were four boys blowing conch trumpets, followed by perhaps ten maidservants surrounding the Queen, who was riding on the back of an elephant and cooling herself with a fan of bird-of-paradise feathers. She was just as the flower guard had said—a radiant beauty, rare in these parts. She couldn't have been more than fourteen or fifteen, but she carried herself with a pride well beyond her years. Seeing this girl, the Prince had to wonder if Kusuko had had a similar way about her when she was that age. And just as that thought occurred to him, his heart skipped a beat. Although the Queen before him was wearing elegant makeup and the finest clothes—suitable indeed for the young wife of a king—he was quite sure he had seen her before.

As she passed, a fragment of memory returned to the Prince, and he let out a small shout. The girl looked so much like a queen, so dignified, that he had almost failed to recognize her. Was the young queen not the tomboy princess of Panpan,

Phatalia Phatata? The Prince forgot all about the pain in his throat and cried out:

"Princess Phatalia Phatata! We meet again!"

The Queen astride her elephant quickly spotted the Prince, opened her eyes wide, and exclaimed in the most delighted voice:

"Oh, Meeko! How I've longed to see you!"

Just hearing Phatalia Phatata's voice was enough to make him cry for joy. The Prince had to wonder if this reunion in the valley wasn't fated from a past life. While the Prince rarely entertained such thoughts, he found himself drawn to this mystical idea.

Princess Phatalia Phatata, daughter of the Governor of Panpan, had come to the nation of Srivijaya as a bride. This kingdom shared the most intimate alliance with her own, and now she was its queen. The two realms were so close that they could easily be mistaken for a single nation. Both were well-known Buddhist kingdoms, but the true nature of their bond was perhaps most evident in the way they jointly governed a number of key posts along the South Sea.

In the interest of accuracy, it's worth mentioning that Princess Phatalia Phatata was now known as Queen Phatalia Phatalia Phatata, as it was the custom in Srivijaya for a married woman to repeat her given name. When she was only a girl, the story goes, the Princess suffered from a terrible melancholy of unknown origin, so she consumed the meat of the baku in her father's menagerie, as recommended by a Brahmin. Even her father and her own handmaidens were convinced that she'd eaten the flesh of the baku and recovered, but in fact she had not. Even the Prince, who was responsible for keeping the baku well fed on pleasant dreams, was entirely unaware of this truth, innocently believing that he and the Princess shared a close connection because she'd eaten the animals that had fed on his dreams.

During her frequent visits to the Garden of Dreams, the Princess had grown attached to the Prince. On occasion, the two of them even strolled through the park, viewing the various birds and beasts together. In those moments, the Princess could hardly have looked any happier. Yet the girl's attachment was even more evident when her father, the Governor of Pan-pan, prepared a ship for the Prince and his fellow travelers so that they could continue their voyage to Hindustan. The Princess stood by her father and pouted as they watched the Prince leave the port of Takkola. Even when the Prince smiled at her, she simply turned away. But perhaps this was just the sort of temperamental display that was to be expected of the Princess.

ABOUT A MONTH HAD passed since the Prince and the Princess were reunited on the valley road. The pain in his throat had become worse in the meantime, and he was bedridden in the seaside hut where he was staying with Anten, Engaku, and Harumaru. All three were deeply concerned. Harumaru begged the Prince with tears in her eyes:

"Miko, you've eaten nothing since yesterday. You've got to keep your strength up. I made some rice porridge with yams. I'm sure it hurts, but you have to try to get something down."

But the Prince replied:

"All signs suggest my death is imminent. It may as well be set in stone. That being the case, there's truly no need for you to worry. Rice and yam porridge has been a favorite of mine from the time I was a boy, but I wonder if the yams will be too much for me. . . . I'm sure I can manage the rice."

When the others' backs were turned, the Prince quickly tossed the food aside, pretending to have eaten it all. Needless to say, Anten, Engaku, and Harumaru were no fools. They knew what the Prince was up to. Still, they knew how painful eating had become for him, so they played along. When morning came, the three of them searched the island for something easier to swallow while the Prince continued to rest alone inside the hut.

During this time, the Prince heard a hesitant tapping at the door and got up to see who it was. It was Princess Phatalia Phatata, but she looked completely different than she had the month before. She was dressed in ordinary clothes and had a worried look on her face.

"I heard about your condition. How are you now? Any better? I was so upset by the news that I simply had to come."

The Prince responded with a smile:

"I'm sure you can tell how I am by the way I sound. There's something stuck in my throat, and it's keeping me from speaking easily. As the days go by, it only gets worse. I'm sure it grates on your ears to listen to a voice like this . . ."

"No, not at all."

"I can barely eat a thing. I know I'm near the end of my life, and I can't say if I will make it to Hindustan before I die. Though ultimately, I would be most pleased if the two events coincided perfectly."

At this, the Princess cried out shrilly:

"You don't say! As it happens, I'm going to die within the year as well. Strange as it may sound, I haven't menstruated since the day we saw each other in the valley."

The Prince couldn't understand what the Princess was saying. What possible relationship could there be between dying and her menses? The Princess took no notice of the Prince's baffled look, however; with a smile on her lips, she took the Prince by the hand and leaned in, whispering in his ear:

"How would you feel about coming with me to the tomb where I will be laid to rest? The location is one that monks from Tang and Hindustan never fail to visit. I suspect you might find it interesting too, Meeko. . . . Well, shall we?"

Although the Prince was quite familiar with the Princess and her whims, he was in no condition to go for a stroll. At the same time, seeing the Princess leap with excitement, he could hardly refuse. The Prince had always had a tendency to yield to the desires of others in this way. So, showing not even a hint of discomfort, he followed the Princess out of the hut. On their way, neither spoke much.

Eventually a hill came into view, upon which stood an imposing structure—a kind of pyramid made of large gray stone blocks. This had to be the tomb. It wasn't much of a hill, but the Prince still found himself short of breath as they made their way up. Perhaps even he hadn't recognized how far his condition had progressed. The view from the top was remarkable: a panorama of fertile plains, and beyond them great volcanoes shooting plumes of white smoke up into the sky. As the Prince took in the incredible view, he completely forgot to wipe the sweat dripping from his brow.

The tomb stood atop five platforms—the bottom three square, the top two round—each of which had an open walkway wrapping around it. There were myriad niches along the walkways, and each contained its own Buddha figure. At the very top of the structure was the tomb, which narrowed toward the tip like a bullet. Having climbed the steep steps, the Prince looked inside and discovered that the tomb was far more spacious than had seemed possible from the outside.

The Princess took his arm, and the Prince tottered into the tomb. It had no windows, and he found it hard to make out his surroundings in the dark. The Princess lit a lantern she had prepared beforehand and held it up to the chamber's curved wall. When she did, a parade of strange figures appeared in a shower of sparks. Life-sized Buddhas, the Prince thought. But, as his eyes adjusted, the Prince recoiled at what he saw. Twenty-two half-naked female figures, all made to look uncannily alive, down to their very pores. They were so lifelike that there was almost something sensuous about them.

The Prince felt his heart jump in his chest, as if he had seen something he should not have. Then the Princess broke the silence:

"Behold the Figures-in-Flesh, the Past Queens of Srivijaya. Each woman succeeded magnificently at bearing a child, thus coming to this tomb in triumph. That is why each face here wears a satisfied smile. The youngest of the queens was seventeen, and the oldest was thirty-one. When I come to this place, I will be far and away the youngest of all. Yes, soon I will have a child and join the other queens in eternal sleep. Ah, how long I've waited to conceive! The shame of not yet being blessed with a child! A wretched curse! My husband was born physically and mentally frail, and I had my doubts that he would ever be able to give me a child. This is why, when you and I crossed paths a month ago, I had gone to visit the Śiva shrine over the mountain. I was praying for an heir. But there's no need for that anymore. Perhaps Śiva answered my prayers. Or perhaps it was you, Meeko. Either way, I haven't had my period since that day . . ."

Now the Prince cut in:

"I'm not sure I understand. Is there some rule in this realm that the queen should die once she's given birth?"

"There is."

"And why is that?"

"I'm not certain myself. I suppose giving birth represents the completion of a woman's life. Beyond that, why go on living? This has been the custom for centuries now, and no queen has ever shirked her duty. On the contrary, they say the queens are more often than not anxious to join the others here in sleep. The same certainly goes for me. What could be better than staying forever young as the youngest yet to complete the queenly task?"

"You say you'll die once you've had a child. . . . But how?"

"Didn't I tell you? In this realm, there is a surefire method for achieving just this. A flower grows in the marshes that feeds on the bodily fluids of human beings, leaving not so much as a drop behind . . ."

"Ah, in that case, I believe I've seen it. A giant red flower, yes?"

"That's right. Should one sit on it, she will soon find herself sapped dry, turned into a perfect mummy. She shall look every bit as she did in life, never showing a hint of age, no matter how many years pass. A flower like this could only blossom in a land in which the Buddha's light shines so brightly, don't you think? It's nothing short of a miracle worker, if you ask me! A Tang monk who passed through the realm not long ago visited this very tomb and was so moved by the sight of these figures that he broke into tears. It seems that in the Tang empire, mummification can only be accomplished through considerable and painstaking work. It involves lacquering and curing and so on. I wonder how it is in Japan. . . . Tell me, Meeko: What is your impression of this tomb?"

"Impression? It's all so incredible, I don't know what to say.

In Japan, there are a few high priests who have become mummies. My own teacher, Kūkai, for example. But I must say I can't name many others who have succeeded in doing so. What's more, I've never heard of a woman doing it! Mount Kōya produces quicksilver, and Kūkai used this to preserve himself . . . I saw him in his coffin—his face in death was almost like a bronze mask."

As the Prince and Princess spoke, they left the dark of the chamber to stand atop the tomb. The sun was shining in the clear sky, and the distant volcanoes were a vivid purple. So high above the ground, the strong breeze made the heat much more tolerable. Sitting on the stone steps, they watched in silence as the undulating columns of smoke rose into the blue sky. After some time, the Princess spoke again:

"Meeko, do you truly wish to make it to Hindustan—even if it costs you your life?"

Startled by the way she phrased her question, the Prince gave the Princess a sidelong glance. She was smiling, but there was a familiar hint of cruelty in her smile. He paid it no mind, however, answering the question as if he wasn't at all disturbed:

"Of course. I have staked everything on getting to Hindustan. I wouldn't mind dying, not in the least."

"So, it makes little difference if you arrive before dying or die before arriving?"

"It would be ideal if they happened to coincide. But, if the chances of that happening are slight, then I suppose it doesn't matter which comes first."

With a twinkle in her eye, the Princess spoke:

"In that case, I have an idea. I'm sure you know the tale of the Buddha sacrificing his own flesh to a hungry tigress, don't you? Being so well read in scripture, you must. Well, if you leave this place and head south, you will soon come to a kingdom across the water, on the northern shore: Luoyue by name. This land has many tigers, all of which travel back and forth between Luoyue and Hindustan—as reliably as migratory birds, never setting so much as a paw astray. Now, as these tigers are very hungry, they are always on the prowl for human flesh, though they wouldn't give a corpse a second look. But if you really don't mind dying on your way to Hindustan, perhaps you should consider surrendering your body to one of these animals, then riding to Hindustan stowed away in its belly. What do you think?"

The Prince's voice leapt right out of his throat:

"Fascinating. It would be like an ox-cart ride to see the sights. I can leave all the traveling to the tiger as I rest inside its stomach—a brilliant plan!"

Their eyes met and they burst out laughing as conspirators might. Then the Princess murmured these words, as if to herself:

"How wonderful! Now Meeko and I are bound to die at the same time. What greater blessing could there be? I'm sure my child will look just like him."

No offense to the Princess, who was wholly convinced that she was going to have a child, but there is a thing in this world called a phantom pregnancy, and it is very common. We shouldn't accept what the Princess said at face value, no matter how much she believed it to be true. Going some time without getting one's period is far from proof that one is pregnant. It's entirely possible that what the Princess believed to be her due date could pass without her ever giving birth—and there would, therefore, be no need for her to die.

Enchanted by the view of the distant volcanoes, the Prince felt more than a little sentimental. He had always had a fondness for great heights—something that Kūkai would never let him live down—yet he was certain this would be the last time he would ever enjoy a view from so high up.

AS SOON AS HE returned to the others, the Prince enthusiastically launched into an explanation of this so-called brilliant plan.

"I have a great idea! I'm going to feed myself to a tiger, and that tiger will then carry me straight to Hindustan in its belly."

Appalled, Anten responded:

"Have you lost your mind? To begin with, where exactly do you hope to find a tiger charitable enough to carry you all the way to Hindustan?"

"Not far from here, as it happens. I'm told that tigers roam the nearby land of Luoyue, then travel homeward to Hindustan. To reach them, I'll simply have to get to Luoyue and find where they gather—easy as that."

"And who on earth gave you this bright idea?"

"Princess Phatalia Phatata. She has a good head on her shoulders, as you know, and is rather knowledgeable when it comes to this part of the world. Little doubt her intelligence on the matter is sound as can be."

The Prince had grown visibly thinner and weaker over the previous few days. With a pained look on his face, Engaku glanced at him and said:

"Whatever the case, you can hardly expect us to stand by and watch as you try to get yourself devoured by a tiger! Miko, I beg you, please stop joking. For you, I would go through fire and water, but this I cannot abide."

Now Harumaru joined the others:

"Even if you were to make it to Hindustan in such a way,

you would arrive as a corpse, trapped in the belly of a beast. That's no way to make an entrance, is it? You'd never be able to see the holy sites at Bodh Gayā, Jetavana, or Nālandā. . . . You'd never hear the cry of the kalaviṅkā. If you can hold on just a little longer, no matter how unwell you are—"

Listening to Harumaru's plea with his eyes closed, the Prince now spoke up:

"No, I'm afraid the reality of things is hardly so forgiving. With my body in this state, there's really no hope of my arriving in Hindustan alive. I'm already so weak. These tigers have no taste for dead flesh, by the way. If I die, the whole plan falls to pieces. I know I've said nothing about it, but this is much more than just a pain in my throat. Simply breathing causes me a great deal of pain, and walking is almost too much to bear. I suppose it would give me some relief to open an air hole in my throat. Not to venture too far into Engaku's territory, but there is a passage in the *Zhuangzi* that reads: 'The true man breathes with his heels while the ordinary man breathes through his throat.' Alas, how badly I wish I had achieved the state of the true man."

The Prince tried to laugh, but what came out was only a miserable growl. At this, the Prince's companions held their heads low. The Prince resumed, now more forcefully:

"Understand that being swallowed by a tiger is not so horrible a fate. We receive life from nature, and we return to it when we die. Isn't it better to sustain the life of a tiger with one's own flesh than to end up in a cold grave? Isn't it much more in keeping with the laws of nature to find my way to Hindustan as part of a tiger? Even Śākyamuni provided us with a splendid example of this when he threw himself to the hungry tigress. How shall I put it? Despite never having seen them, I already feel a certain sympathy with the tigers of Luoyue."

After several days, four magnificent elephants arrived from the court of Srivijaya. They were surely a nudge from the Princess, meant to carry the Prince and his three companions to Luoyue. To get there, however, the travelers would first need to journey some two hundred li south over the Isle of Sumatra, to the point where the Malay Peninsula was easiest to access by ship. Luoyue stood at the southern tip of that peninsula. At this time, it was one of a number of small nations thriving along the South Sea trade route. This was likely all the travelers would have known about Luoyue as they set out in that direction.

On the morning of their departure, the Prince lay on his straw mat, his shoulders heaving with each breath. In a voice like that of a mosquito, he spoke to his companions:

"Suppose I might be granted a single request today. Could one of you bring me a small round object? Something I can hold in the palm of my hand? Really, any pebble will do . . ."

"As you wish," Harumaru answered and got right up. It took her only a couple of minutes to fetch a good-sized stone, but by the time she returned, the Prince had already drifted off to sleep. Softly, she said:

"Miko, here's the stone you asked for . . ."

At her voice, the Prince slowly opened his eyes.

"Ah, right. I almost forgot. Would you mind helping me up?"

Anten propped him up against the pile of straw, and then the Prince continued:

"Now will you place that stone in my right hand? Yes, just like that . . ."

The Prince gripped the stone firmly, held it up high, and made a motion as if he were about to toss it as far as he could. He did this not once but many times. Then, as if singing:

"Away, away you go! Off to distant Hindustan!"

The others watched in shock, wondering if the Prince had finally lost his mind. Engaku bit down hard on his lip as though on the verge of breaking down.

While the Prince repeated that motion, he kept the stone in his hand. Then, almost as if he had lost interest in the thing, he dropped it onto the floor of the hut, lay down again, and shut his eyes. Anten leaned in and casually asked:

"What was that you did with the stone just now? Some sort of spell?"

With a faint smile on his lips, the Prince replied:

"No, no. Nothing like that. As you know, when I was only a boy, I was quite close to the infamous Fujiwara no Kusuko. There was a time when she threw a ball of light into the courtyard at night. It's something I've never been able to forget. Remembering it now as I was nodding off, I thought I should give it a try . . ."

"And how was it?"

"I couldn't really tell you, to be honest. How strange. . . . It makes me wonder why that episode has been so firmly lodged in my mind these many decades. I always wanted to try it for myself, just once before I died . . ."

As he spoke, the Prince began to drift off again. His companions looked on in concern. Then, after some time, the Prince said:

"So sorry, would you help me up again? Princess Phatalia Phatata is here."

The Prince was apparently asleep—or so they thought. After all, the Princess was nowhere to be seen. Still, as soon as he spoke, Anten wasted no time sitting him up against the straw. The Prince was now upright, even though he looked far from awake. In fact, he seemed to be wandering the depths of sleep—dreaming.

Let's change our perspective now and enter the Prince's dream along with Princess Phatalia Phatata.

Slithering into the hut like a snake, the Princess went right up to the Prince and whispered:

"Does your throat feel any better?"

The Prince looked up, his back still against the straw, where Anten had placed him.

"It's even worse. It's this pearl. No matter what I do, it won't come loose. It's stuck. See how swollen my throat is? Here, feel for yourself."

The Princess brushed the side of the Prince's neck with her slender fingers, then lowered her voice and said:

"As you can see, my fingers are long and thin. If you'd like, I can reach down your throat and pull the pearl out."

Like a child, the Prince gave a spirited nod.

The girl's white fingers appeared to be twice as long as those of an ordinary person. Her fingernails were very long too, and beautifully polished like agates. As her fingers approached the Prince's eyes, they seemed to him like insectivorous vines reaching for their prey. Although he was a little frightened, he opened his mouth obediently and allowed the girl's fingers to enter his throat.

It could not have gone more smoothly. The Princess inserted her fingers deep into the Prince's throat and swiftly pulled out the glowing sphere, a grin spreading across her face as she held up the troublesome object. The Prince couldn't take his eyes off it. He simply stared in amazement at the pearl that had been trapped in his throat all that time.

"Well, how's that? Better?"

As a matter of fact, yes. The Prince felt much better now. He was breathing easily again. What a relief, he thought, when the Princess began to speak—and her words struck him like a whip:

"This pearl will kill you, Meeko. Yet look at its beauty. It can be yours, but then there can be no escape from death. If you mean to escape death, you must let go of the pearl. Which will it be? You may choose only one, and the choice is yours to make."

Oddly, the voice the Prince heard was no longer that of the Princess. In fact, he thought he recognized Kusuko's knowing tone. The Princess no longer looked like herself either; had she transformed into Kusuko? When had that happened? Even the Prince could not say. Like any dreamer, the Prince was not necessarily aware that a transformation had taken place. So how could anyone else have known? Suffice it to say that such things often occur in dreams.

Now Kusuko rose to her feet. She held up the pearl in her right hand, but the object was now the size of a pebble and glowing even brighter.

"All is well, Meeko. No need to worry. Once your life ends in this world, this ball of light will fly across the sea to Japan, where your life force will begin anew. Meanwhile, your spirit will be free to wander Hindustan eternally."

Glancing for a moment at Anten and Engaku, Kusuko lifted her arm up slowly and hurled the shining stone toward the doorway.

"Away, away you go! Off to Japan!"

The stone flew past the earthen walls of the hut, grazing the tips of the palm fronds outside as it drew a luminous arc through the sky and into the distance. In that same instant, Kusuko vanished.

The Prince immediately collapsed onto the pallet of straw. The others, who had been watching him closely, believed this might be the end of him. They hurried to his side to examine his face. Yet what they found was a look of profound peace. At this, they breathed a collective sigh of relief. Engaku folded his arms and said, as if to himself:

"How strange. . . . Is that the scent of a woman? Was someone here just now?"

Of course, not having been inside the Prince's dream, his companions had missed Kusuko and the Princess entirely. How can anyone know what's happening in someone else's dream?

One more thing, however, would continue to bother Engaku. Despite thoroughly searching the hut, he could not find the stone that Harumaru had fetched for the Prince. Perhaps someone had tossed it outside—but who?

ON THE MORNING OF their departure, when the others helped him onto his elephant, the Prince appeared to be in high spirits for what seemed like the first time in ages. A howdah just big enough for him to lie on comfortably had been mounted on the elephant's back. It seemed that Princess Phatalia Phatata had thought of everything. While in his dreams the Prince had made a miraculous recovery, the pain was the same as ever once he awoke. Nevertheless, he was so excited about the journey ahead that he appeared to have forgotten all about his condition.

There's no need to go into the minutiae of the journey to Luoyue. The travelers headed south along the eastern extremes of Sumatra. This vast marshland was nothing like the volcanic regions to the west, and passage through these parts would have been virtually impossible without the aid of the elephants. Again, the monks had to appreciate the Princess and her thorough preparations. The journey took more than three months, at which point the Strait of Malacca came into view. At this sight, the travelers—still astride their muddy elephants—felt as if they had at last been brought back to life. Here they abandoned the elephants and hired a small boat that took them to Singapura on the opposite coast. They were now in Luoyue.

Contrary to expectation, Singapura was desolate and overrun with dense tropical plant life. There were what appeared to be the stony remains of an ancient port, but the wave-washed rock clearly no longer served any purpose. Now the travelers understood the faces the locals had made when they asked for a boat. According to these locals, the tigers would come to the tip of the Malay Peninsula, then swim to the island by way of the Straits of Johor.

The night of their arrival, the Prince went off alone to find what he deemed the most suitable grove, where he lay down in the grass. He passed the night repeating the treasured name of Maitreya, the Buddha of the Future, waiting for a tiger to discover him, but no such animal appeared. In the morning, the Prince returned to his companions where they were waiting and said with a wry smile:

"Even dying has proven more difficult than expected. But tomorrow, I'm sure, will be my day . . ."

The next night, the moon was once again shining brightly —all the land was bathed in its light. When the Prince left camp, the others began to chant Maitreya's name, and continued until morning. No doubt they would have been unable to sleep even had they tried. They waited and waited for the Prince, yet even when morning came, he did not return.

The three of them looked at one another and nodded in

agreement. They went to the grove where the Prince had been, but he was gone. There were only a few blood-spattered bones to greet them, glinting in the white light of morning.

"Oh, the sadness! Oh, the sadness! The world has never known such sadness! The Prince is dead!"

Anten fell to his knees and beat the earth with his fists, sobbing uncontrollably. Engaku grabbed hold of a nearby tree and shook it with all his might.

Then came a cry, clear and shrill, hurtling through the air like a rainbow. In the same moment, the monks saw a small olive-colored bird rise up from among the grasses and twirl into the sky.

*Meee-ko! Meee-ko! Meee-ko!*

A nightingale? But its face was unmistakably Harumaru's. The bird's round eyes were brimming with tears as it flew off, following the tiger toward Hindustan, like as not. Anten and Engaku stood there in a daze, tracing the bird's flight with their eyes, paying no mind to the bloody bones at their feet.

*Meee-ko! Meee-ko! Meee-ko!*

The bird was now little more than a dark dot in the distant sky, but its beautiful cry lingered.

"That can only be the kalaviṅkā. Hearing its cry is as good as having reached Hindustan."

At last, the two monks returned their gaze to the Prince's bones and gathered them in silence. The bones were as thin and light as fiberglass. How fitting for a Prince as modern as Takaoka.

While it cannot be confirmed, Prince Takaoka is believed to have died at the end of the sixth year of the Xiantong era—Jōgan 7 by the Japanese calendar. He was then sixty-five years of age. Although it may have seemed that the Prince visited a great many lands and seas since leaving Guangzhou, not even a full year had passed since his departure.

# TRANSLATOR'S AFTERWORD

## Who Was Prince Takaoka?

*Takaoka's Travels* (*Takaoka shinnō kōkaiki*) follows Prince Taka-oka as he makes his way across Asia, but the novel eschews linear progress in favor of a spiral structure. As Patrick Honnoré writes in the preface to his French translation of the book, Shibusawa's novel might as well have been titled "Prince Takaoka, or Limbo in the Indian Ocean."

The historical Prince Takaoka, who lived in the ninth century, lost his status in the courtly world of Kyoto after his father conspired against the sitting emperor. Following the example of disgraced princes who came before him, Takaoka then became a Buddhist monk. Later in life, when he was in his sixties, the Prince left Japan. According to *Le Dictionnaire historique du Japon*:

> Takaoka decided to go to China to study under the masters. [. . .] After three years, however, he had not found what he was looking for, so he left with the intention of going to India. But he died before reaching his destination, in the kingdom of Luoyue, in the vicinity of present-day Singapore. The Prince was nonetheless the first

Japanese person of his time to venture so far to
the west.

Shibusawa no doubt did his homework when writing
*Takaoka's Travels*, but the narrative swiftly moves beyond documented history. At its heart, the novel is a fantasy, and, as the
writer Katsuhiko Takahashi has noted, the majority of the story
takes place within dreams—or dreams within dreams.

Even when the Prince isn't dreaming, he and his retinue
encounter miracles and anachronisms at every turn. While the
monks accompanying Takaoka are understandably frustrated
by these supernatural developments, the Prince revels in them.

Yet at some point, Takaoka's journey takes a dark turn.
The Prince begins to suspect that he will die before arriving
at his destination. In the novel's penultimate chapter, this suspicion becomes all-consuming. The Prince swallows a pearl
that robs him of his health and his voice. Then, in the final
chapter, we are led to believe that he has fed himself to a tiger
bound for the birthplace of the Buddha. This is not, of course,
an unhappy ending. While the Prince is unable to witness the
glory of the holy land with his own eyes, Shibusawa suggests
that he will nevertheless arrive—in some form—in the land of
his dreams.

It's worth mentioning here that the end of Takaoka's life is
made to mirror that of the author. Shibusawa was dying as he
wrote this book. He had laryngeal cancer, and had to have his
vocal cords removed. Toward the end of his life, he could com-
municate only through writing. He had died by the time *Takaoka's Travels* won the Yomiuri Prize in 1987.

### Who Was Tatsuhiko Shibusawa?

> Some boys go through a phase in which they
> find it impossible to think about anything but
> bug-hunting or collecting plants. They'll take one
> look at the assignments they're supposed to com-
> plete over summer vacation, see the word speci-
> men, and turn in the most elaborately assembled
> case — all the while ignoring every other piece of
> homework. I imagine everybody had a collector
> or two like this in their class. Tatsuhiko Shibu-
> sawa strikes me as one of these boys.
> —Takaaki Yoshimoto (1924–2012)

Tatsuhiko Shibusawa (1928–1987) first made a name for himself in the fifties as a translator of Jean Cocteau and several other French writers. What made him a star in literary circles, however, was his behavior in what came to be known as "The Sade Trial."

In 1959, Shibusawa and his publisher were taken to court for their translation of the Marquis de Sade's novel *L'Histoire de Juliette ou les Prospérités du vice*, which had been published in two volumes under the title *Akutoku no sakae* (Vice amply rewarded).

This was postwar Japan's second obscenity trial. Translator and author Sei Itō had faced the same charge roughly a decade earlier for his translation of D.H. Lawrence's *Lady Chatterley's Lover*.

Both Itō and Shibusawa were eventually found guilty, but the prosecutors claimed that the two translators were at fault for very different reasons. Itō was accused of being, if anything, too faithful to Lawrence's English, whereas Shibusawa—having deliberately trimmed away the more soporific passages in *Juliette*—was accused of taking Sade's work into his own hands and making the obscene work even more obscene in translation.

Moreover, Itō had appeared in court wearing a double-breasted suit, playing the part of the repentant defendant, but Shibusawa strolled into court wearing sunglasses and smoking a pipe—if, that is, he bothered showing up at all. He used his time in the national spotlight to ridicule his accusers, which quickly won him the admiration of the literary world as well as the general public.

In the decades that followed, Shibusawa established himself as one of Japan's most shocking and powerful voices. He continued his work as a translator, and also published essays on subjects that polite society would rather ignore—everything from alchemy to torture. As poet and critic Takaaki Yoshimoto suggested in his 1962 review of Shibusawa's work, the author was a collector by nature, an "insect boy" (*konchū shōnen*) who used the essay form as a literary specimen case. Needless to say, we can find a similar orientation in *Takaoka's Travels*, Shibusawa's only full-length novel. As a close friend of the author's once told me, this book is best read as a "cabinet of curiosities"—a record of a lifelong obsession with all things strange and exotic.

WITH THE EXCEPTION OF the short story "Gyorinki," translated by Anthony Chambers in 1987 as "Fish Scales," this book represents Shibusawa's first work available in English.

I've been living with this translation for a very long time, and I'd like to take this opportunity to thank the mentors, friends, and colleagues who have read and discussed Shibusawa's work with me over the years.

First and foremost, I want to thank Motoyuki Shibata for showing me how to translate—and how to translate with heart.

I could not have translated this book without the advice and support that I received from Shun'ichirō Akikusa, Kay Duffy, Ted Goossen, Elijah Greenstein, Kaoru Hayashi, Osamu Ikeuchi, Madoka Kishi, Ryan S. Morrison, Fukumi Nihira, Mitsuyoshi Numano, Keiko Ono, Hiroshi Takayama, and Evan Young.

During revisions over the past few years, Sam Bett and Daniel Joseph helped me to find depth and humor that I hadn't captured in early drafts. Asa Yoneda showed me greater potential in every word, and the spaces in between.

I'd also like to thank Chance Cockrell for his careful eye, and Maren Ehlers, Emek Ergun, Phil Kaffen, Alexandra Kaloyanides, and Ritika Prasad at the University of North Carolina at Charlotte for offering feedback on parts of the book in draft form.

My heartfelt thanks to my teachers Etsuko Sakurai and Hiroko Ōtake, and to my parents, Vicki and Rocky Hildebrandt.

It's been a joy working on this book with Ruth Gaskill, Peter Goodman, and—of course—Meg Taylor. Having the right editor makes all the difference.

Finally, this translation would not have been possible without Ryūko Shibusawa, who generously met with me on multiple occasions to discuss her late husband's work.

I WOULD LIKE TO borrow a few of Shibusawa's own words from the afterword to *Sakashima*, his 1962 translation of *À rebours* by J.K. Huysmans, to convey my feelings about translating this novel: "I've never struggled with a translation so much before. Then again, while it was certainly a struggle, I doubt I've ever enjoyed translating a book so much."

## ABOUT THE AUTHOR AND TRANSLATOR

**TATSUHIKO SHIBUSAWA** (1928–1987) published only one novel, *Takaoka's Travels*, but it is considered a touchstone of Japanese counterculture. He was a prolific translator of French literature, known for his translations of the Marquis de Sade and the surrealists. In addition to *Takaoka's Travels*, he published several volumes of short fiction and numerous essays dealing with topics ranging from dreams to the occult.

**DAVID BOYD** is an award-winning translator of modern and contemporary Japanese literature. He has translated fiction by Hiroko Oyamada, Mieko Kawakami, Izumi Suzuki, and Toh EnJoe, among many others. He teaches translation at the University of North Carolina at Charlotte.